CORY
Two Trees

by

ED STAUFFER

ISBN 978-1-956001-29-7 (paperback)
ISBN 978-1-956001-30-3 (eBook)

Chapter 1

It was a warm late spring night. State Trooper Jacob (Jake) Cooke sat in his patrol car watching for speeders on the moonless night. Windows open, he felt the warm breeze waft through the car. There must have been a blooming bush or flowers nearby because occasionally, he could detect a slight sweet aroma. There wasn't much traffic on Deer Creek Road, and he wondered to himself why he was assigned to it. He had not stopped even one speeder and when he thought about the traffic, he believed in the past hour he did not see more than a total of six cars drive by in either directions. No matter. In another half hour, his shift would be over, turn in his patrol car and he would be able to go home. Made him think about who might greet him at the door of her apartment, Deidre. He wouldn't be going home. No. So, he sat. He thought about his newest girlfriend and the trouble her mother was making for them both, especially Deidre. Her mother complained about his womanizing. He blamed her for his reason, seeing other women, but tonight his newest girlfriend would be waiting for him. Different thoughts of several of his past romances raced through his mind as he waited. He thought about Sue Ellen and why he left her. Left her for B. J. But he soon tired of her and his mind jumped from one thought to another. He asked himself, why doesn't he marry Deidre? Could he, would he be faithful? Yes, he thought. Why didn't her mother mind her own business? Could he stand her if she became his mother-in-law? He would have to learn how to avoid her.

His thoughts shifted back to why he was here, he could see a car's headlights approaching him. He looked down at his radar gun screen and was mildly surprised and pleased to see that the approaching car was traveling almost eighty miles per hour as it sped past him. Since Deer Creek Road was made up of several curves it was for the most part posted at forty-five. Jake started his patrol car, flipped on his siren and police car lights and pulled onto the road and raced after the miscreant.

After a quarter mile chase, the speeder pulled to the side of the road. He quickly typed into his car's computer what he thought was the license plate since it was partially covered with mud and saw a response that they were legitimate. The owner didn't have a warrant out for him nor that he has any traffic infringements. Jake made sure his car's camera and its audio were both on and working, he wanted it documented if the speeder was drunk and vocal and that he didn't do anything improper. Hand on his holster, he got out of his patrol car and walked toward the speeder. He knocked on the car's window and signaled that the driver should open it. When the window was down, Jake placed one hand on the windowsill and leaned toward the open window. His patrol car camera's audio picked him up as he told the driver to turn the car off and began to say that he needed to see the driver's car registration and driving license. The patrolman's face registered shock at what he saw in the car, but he had no time to respond as he was quickly shot three times in the chest. Jake pitched backward and fell onto his back on the road. The speeder raced off as his patrol car's camera showed a pool of blood forming around the shot trooper. Each time the patrol car lights switched to blue, the blood turned black. It exaggerated the situation, the shot trooper.

Several minutes passed before a car's headlights approached from the direction that the speeder had gone. The car pulled to the side of the road and a young man followed by a woman got out and went to the shot trooper. A quick look at the trooper in the pool of blood that had pooled around him, he turned and told the woman to call 911. She returned to their car, grabbed a cell phone from her purse and dialed.

It took over five minutes before the couple could hear in the distance the wail of sirens and soon they could see flashing police and emergency rescue lights approach. A sheriff's deputy car came into view and it was followed by a state trooper's car. A fire and rescue van brought up the rear and when the sheriff and trooper stopped the fire and rescue van drove past them to the shot trooper. Three EMT's jumped out of the van and went to the shot trooper. One tried CPR, another took his blood pressure and the third gave him a shot of something. They waited, listened to his heart. Eventually they stood up, the first one looked at the deputy sheriff and shook his head no. He said, "Never had a chance. Looks like a large caliber gun and one hit him in the heart." One of the EMT's covered the body with a sheet.

The three vehicles would be followed with additional police, emergency and the morgue vehicles. Soon the scene was crowded with about twenty various law enforcement officers. Two were sent to close the road in both directions.

The following morning in the roll call room of the county sheriff's office, plain clothes and uniformed deputy sheriff's officers were gathered around the TV monitor. The news caster was finishing up on her report of last night's trooper shooting. "… and just outside of the city of Westover, State Trooper Jake Cooke was shot and killed in what was believed a simple speeding stop. The shooter was driving a blue 1990's Ford Escort Sedan. Anyone with information concerning the car or shooting should please call their local police or sheriff's office. Elsewhere a local…" Sergeant Albert Light turned the TV off, turned and walked to his podium. All the gathered force waited for his morning roll call and assignments. Everyone was to continue what they had been doing the day before. There were no special assignments, but all were told to keep an eye out for the blue ford mentioned on the news cast.

Plain clothes Deputy Sheriff Jesus (JC) Cardozza asked, "Who of us will get the case? Will we investigate?"

"No," said Sheriff's Deputy Billy Bob (BB) Larkin, a large black fellow plain clothes deputy, "The state police will want to handle it, keep it in house."

"But it happened in our jurisdiction, we should be investigating it," Deputy JC Cardozza said to BB.

Sergeant Light said, "It may be in our jurisdiction, but they will want to handle it. They are bigger, say the state is their jurisdiction, they have more resources and will throw their weight around."

"If we are lucky, they may ask us for help, maybe run-down leads and some minor stuff," Deputy BB Larkin replied.

Sergeant Light continued, "The ME technician in the morgue told me that he had been shot three times in the chest with a .45 caliber pistol."

"Were they able to recover any of the slugs?" Deputy JC Cardozza wanted to know.

"Two mushroomed, impossible to trace them if we find the gun, but the third went through a lot of soft tissue, missed a rib and through the heart, and is in perfect condition. If they find the gun CSI will be able to match it," Sergeant Light told the group.

"We should be so lucky," Deputy JC Cardozza replied.

Deputy BB Larkin said, "Like I said, they will ask for help if they need it. Odds are, they will not."

At the end of the roll call, the sergeant said before he dismissed everyone, the sheriff wished to talk to them. He talked into his shoulder microphone. The deputies quietly talked among themselves. A minute later county Sheriff Frank Cooper entered the room. He was not a big man, but he carried himself well and looked impressive.

"Okay, okay, everyone quit down," Sergeant Light said.

The sheriff went to the podium and addressed his men. "I think you all heard about the state trooper being shot. I have just gotten off the telephone with Captain Meyers of the state police. We will not be involved in the investigation, but if we should run across anything we should give them a heads up."

Deputy BB Larkin said loud enough for all to hear, "Just as I thought."

Deputy JC Cardozza couldn't keep quiet, "I suppose they will be very appreciative."

"Yes, well, we all have our own work to do, so let's do it," the sheriff replied. He then handed the meeting back to the sergeant who dismissed the officers.

Chapter 2

It was the afternoon of that day when the sheriff's receptionist, Linda Lee, knocked on his open-door. Not looking up the sheriff motioned her to enter. When she did, Ms. Lee pulled the door closed behind her. Sheriff Cooper looked up at her when he heard the door close and asked what she wanted. "Sheriff, I received a call that a woman walking her dog found a dead body in the Oak Ridge Drive at the Oak Estates area. I sent Fred Johnston and Jesus Cardozza to check it out. I was a little surprised that Fred didn't want to talk about it over the radio but telephoned. He is on the phone and wants to talk to you."

Sheriff Cooper picked up the phone and pushed the flashing button. "This is Cooper, what is it Fred?"

He heard Deputy Fred Johnston say, "I didn't want to call it in on our radio. We found a dead woman, Connie Brookfield. She was on the side of the road, not visible from the car. The woman who found her was waiting for us and pointed her out. She looks like a hit and run."

"Jesus!" the sheriff uttered.

"How do you want to handle this?" Fred asked.

The following morning Sheriff Cooper was addressing his officers at the morning roll call. "Connie Brookfield was killed by a hit and run driver. The ME said that she had been hit the day before yesterday. All the ME and CSI could tell me was that she was hit by a light blue vehicle. The small portion of paint on her is being analyzed and hopefully will tell us the make and year of the car. Our night duty sergeant, Will Belfry at the desk, said her husband Brooks, called two nights ago to report her missing. Wanted to file a missing person report. Said she did not return from her usual evening run. Will told him he would have to wait two days. I don't have to tell you that her husband Brooks is a close friend to both the mayor and governor. The quicker we can find the driver, the better it will be for all of us."

Deputy Susan Black asked, "Anything else we should know?"

Sheriff Cooper continued, "The ME believes she was hit on the driver's side in the back and on the wrong side of the road. The driver was going at a very fast rate of speed. From where CSI believe she was hit to where she was found was close to a hundred feet. They couldn't find any skid marks. The driver made no attempt to brake. She couldn't be seen from the road, wouldn't have been found if the pedestrian hadn't spotted her. We will check everywhere in the city as well as the county, all garages or auto repair shops for blue cars needing repair. Any blue cars sold for junk. Check all the local bars, anyone who stood out as drunk in the late afternoon or are known to be heavy day drinkers. Anyone who has a current DUI."

"I'd like to start with her husband," Deputy Cory Two Trees responded.

"No, we stay away from him," Sheriff Cooper replied. "Right now, he is not a suspect."

Deputy Two Trees continued, "Shouldn't we at least eliminate him as a suspect?"

"No! Fred Johnston and his partner Jesus Cardozza will lead the investigation," replied the sheriff. "Everyone, no matter how small the lead, follow up on it by running it past Fred or his partner," the sheriff motioned to both of them, "and the two of you keep me up to date and informed. I know I'm going to have to answer to a lot of people. Before you break for the day's assignments, Cory, I want to talk to you in my office."

Deputy Johnston asked, "Any questions?" When there weren't any he said, "JC and I will be giving you temporary assignments and areas to cover."

In the sheriff's office, the sheriff sat and looked across his desk at Deputy Two Trees. He saw what he considered a rugged good-looking young man, six feet tall with jet black hair without any distinguishing features. He was of dark complexion and could pass for half dozen different nationalities. If the sheriff didn't know his father was a native American Indian and that Deputy Two Trees was from the Colville reservation, he would never consider him to be half Indian. Before he joined the county sheriff's department, all the sheriff knew about him was after he graduated from college he applied to police training. When asked why he wanted to be in law enforcement he wrote that he thought it was a noble profession and that his father had been a policeman and killed on the job. Asked why the sheriff deputy department, he said it didn't want to be confined to a desk. "Stay clear of Brooks, is that understood?" the sheriff said.

All that Deputy Two Trees could say was a humble, "Yes."

When he was sure that his deputy heard him and understood, the sheriff said, "The two of you have had words. He called you a half breed who lied about his client. He may have apologized and withdrew his statement, but the jury heard him, and he was not believed. The result was his client was convicted. I don't think he has ever forgiven you for that."

Deputy Two Trees replied, "He is the problem, not me. I've been called worse. I've almost forgotten the whole thing, and I didn't lie."

"I believe you," replied the sheriff, "but I believe he blames you for making him lose control and use what the newspaper called a racist comment. I intend to make sure you stay away from him. I want you to talk to the Corilla family. They reported their daughter missing, kidnapped. Deputies Breem and Reese told me and the family that she is most likely a run-away. They could not find anything that told them otherwise. I've taken the two off the case and assigned them to the hit and run. I want you to check out the missing girl and get back to me. Mr. Corilla keeps calling. He is half of Ford and Corilla Real Estate. He is a big contributor to city politics. I've had at least one city councilman call and ask how the investigation is going. Most likely the city councilman is a friend of Mr. Corilla. I know that when you start an investigation you'll not let it go until you find an ending. Go where the evidence takes you. One way or the other, I'd like some closure on this. If she is a run-away, find something to prove it."

He gave the sheriff a believable, "Yes sir," turned and left the sheriff's office.

Deputy Two Trees drove to the address of the Corilla family. He thought that he would want to first look at Brooks. But the sheriff may have assigned him to this simple go nowhere run-away case. It would keep him away from Brooks. Maybe it was the correct assignment. He found the Corilla house just inside the city limits in an area being developed. It was one of several new homes that were built, and it was surrounded be a well-manicured lawn with flowers near the house. He rang the bell, introduced himself, showed his credentials and was invited into the Corilla home. He saw a new, upper middle-class home with what he thought had a Mexican feel, Mexican paintings, rugs, a display of guitars and several paintings of saints. He introduced himself to Mr. and Mrs. Corilla. He assumed the two others were members of the family, but they were not introduced. The family invited the deputy to sit at the dining room table and they all joined him. "Deputies Breem and Reese have been reassigned. I am taking over their case. Since I am new, you will need to bring me up to date. I have Deputy Breem's notes from their investigation, but I would rather hear it from you. I'll start with his note, the last time you saw your daughter Angelina, was over a week ago on Wednesday when she left to join her friends at the mall on the east side of town. Can either of you add anything to that?"

Before they could answer, the young man who was not introduced spoke up. The deputy saw a scrawny young man with both arms tattooed and before either Mr. or Mrs. Corilla could say anything, the young man said, "Why'd them white dudes taken off the case!? And there were two of them. Don't we rate!?"

"Detective Breem and his partner said there was no ransom note or call. Has that changed?" Deputy Two Trees asked and dismissed the question asked.

"That's right, when we last saw her, and no, there has been nothing from or about her," Mr. Corilla replied.

The young man directed his next comment toward Deputy Two Trees and demanded, "You heard me! Well?"

Mrs. Corilla said, "Let's listen to the deputy Juan."

After the last remark Deputy Two Trees asked, "Your name is Juan?"

"That's right," Juan replied.

"What is your full name?" Deputy Two Trees asked. Before Juan could answer he took out a pen and was ready to write in the margin of Deputy Breem's report.

"Juan-Hernando Medina," he answered.

"Since you are not part of the family, what is your relationship to Angelina?" Deputy Two Trees wanted to know.

"No relation, a concerned friend," Juan replied.

Because Juan had been introduced Deputy Two Trees turned his attention to the young woman. He saw a beautiful woman, dark hair, perfect white teeth, dark eyes and when she smiled, cute dimples. He thought to himself that she was quite shapely. Before he could ask her, he heard, "I'm her sister Carmen. Juan-Hernando Medina is a good family friend."

While he was writing Mrs. Corilla said, "Angelina is a good girl. She got along well with everyone and was well liked by her friends. Attended church every Sunday."

"She just turned fourteen, a week later she disappears. She was never in trouble, never argued with us and never stayed out past curfew," Mr. Corilla added.

"What are you going to do about her!?" asked Juan before deputy Two Trees could answer.

Deputy Two Trees ignored Juan's request. "Did she have a boyfriend Mrs. Corilla? There is no mention of one in the initial report."

Without hesitation Mrs. Corilla said, "She's too young to be dating and I wouldn't allow it. She mostly hung out with her girlfriends."

"What does a boyfriend have to do with her being kidnapped!?" Juan demanded to know.

Deputy Two Trees turned his attention to Juan and said, "Please, let me ask the questions Mr. Medina. It's possible if she had a boyfriend she could have run off with him."

"No! No! No boyfriend," Mrs. Corilla almost shouted. "She didn't run away!"

"Some of her girlfriends' names," he asked.

"You think her girlfriends are involved?" asked Juan.

"No, but I have to start somewhere." He turned away from Juan and looked at Mrs. Corilla. "Can you give me their names? I have them here in Deputy Breem's report, but I want to hear their names from you." Deputy Two Trees thought that maybe they would mention a friend's name that the original investigating deputies did not receive.

Carmen Corilla said, "There is Christy Miller, Brandy something, don't know her last name. Then there is Bonita Escadillo and Candice Williams that I know of. They can tell you if there are others."

Deputy Two Trees wrote the names down and turned toward Juan and said, "Before you open your mouth again, let me explain to you and the family what I'm doing. The original deputies investigating her missing filed their report as a possible run-away. They didn't find a diary that may have given a hint to where she would run away to or mention a boy she may have been seeing. Someone who may have been following her."

Carmen Corilla spoke, "That's right. As far as I know she didn't have a diary."

"That closed the case for a while," Deputy Two Trees said. "I've been reassigned to the case. I'll be looking at everything with fresh eyes and may find something that they may have missed. So please forgive me if I ask questions you've already answered, or if I offend you with the questions."

"I, we, want to see some results!" Juan was quick to add.

"I can either stop and let it be as a simple run-away or proceed." He addressed the four of them and waited for an answer.

Carmen didn't hesitate, "Don't open your mouth Juan! Go ahead deputy, continue."

"Anything else that you can think of that might be a lead?" he asked.

Mrs. Corilla answered, "She did baby sit quit a few times for the Myrinces. They live in the Belford development area." Deputy Two Trees saw the Myrince name in the original investigation report.

"She did stay out several times past curfew, but nothing serious. She always was with her friends or the Myrinces didn't come home on time."

"So, there were times that she stayed out past her curfew," the deputy remarked.

"Yes, but not serious enough for us to punish her or question her about," Mrs. Corilla answered.

"Being only fourteen, how did she get to these places?" he wanted to know.

"One of her two friends old enough to drive would pick her up and I drove her to the Myrince's twice. They live less than a half mile from here, so she would walk home, or Mr. Myrince would drop her off," Mr. Corilla said. "On the Wednesday that she disappeared, one of her girlfriends came by and got her."

"Do you remember which one?" He heard Mrs. Corilla utter a no. He remembered reading in Deputy Breem's report that Mrs. Corilla believed it was Christy. He would follow up on that. "And you are sure she didn't have a boyfriend? How about a boy she may have been friendly with?" he wanted to know. Again Mrs. Corilla was sure there were neither. "Do you know if she drank or did drugs?"

"Absolutely no! We would have known. She was too interested in sports," Mrs. Corilla said.

Juan with skepticism in his voice asked, "You think she was a druggie?"

"No," he replied, "but I have to ask. Sometimes the family is the last to know. Do you have a recent photo of her?"

Mrs. Corilla got up and went into the living room and soon returned with a photograph. "Here is her school picture."

Deputy Two Trees looked at it and then at Carmen and commented, "She is quite beautiful, and she is only fourteen years old? You may be her sister but you two could pass as twins, definitely sisters."

Carmen blushed slightly at the comment and replied, "Yes. I've been with her when she has passed for twenty, but she is ten years younger than me."

Not to be left out of the conversation Juan said, "Guys did want to date her."

"How do you know that?" Deputy Two Trees asked.

"I'd been asked to help fix them up with a date," he replied.

"Why didn't you tell us that Juan?" Mrs. Corilla asked.

Juan didn't answer, so Deputy Two Trees asked, "Did you?"

Juan was quick to reply, "No!"

"I'd like their names," and he prepared to write what Juan told him.

Instead, Juan said, "I'm not going to get a few of my *amigos* investigated."

"Do you think that any of them would have anything to hide?" asked Deputy Two Trees.

Juan hesitated before he answered, "No. I made it up, No one asked me."

"Tell him!" Carmen demanded.

"Their names and addresses! I'm not going to ask again," deputy Two Trees said, and he could see the determined look on Carmen's face when she looked at Juan.

"Ronny Lopez," he finally was able to utter.

"Who else?"

"Three Fingers Lopez," Juan added. "They are cousins."

"What's his first name?" Deputy Two Trees wanted to know.

"That's it. Never heard him called anything else cause he lost two fingers in a playground accident," Juan said.

"Are we going to be her all day?" Deputy Two Trees was getting impatient. "Who else?"

"Hector Escadillo. That's all," Juan said with finality.

Deputy Two Trees had to ask, "Is he related to Bonita?"

"Yes, she is his sister. If you question them, do you have to mention my name?" Juan wanted to know.

"I'll try to keep your name out of it. Now, where can I find these three young men?"

Juan fidgeted. Deputy Two Trees believed he acted like he needed a cigarette. He would not give up on what Juan had told him and stared at Juan, he waited for an answer, "They hang out as a group, usually at *El Rancho,* Mexican restaurant on third street."

"I know the other deputies were wrong, Angelina did not run away. She has been kidnapped," Mrs. Corilla said.

He believed he got all that he could from the Corilla family, Deputy Two Trees got up to leave and told them he would do his best to find her. As protective of their daughter and the young woman they believed her to be, he did not ask the question that would need to be asked, could she have been pregnant? A big reason many young girls run away. If the family was as protective of her as he believed, most likely no. Maybe one of her friends would have known. He would follow up on that. He made no promises and said he'd keep in touch and he left.

Chapter 3

The following morning the sheriff was addressing his men. "Listen up. Fred is going to bring everyone up to date on the hit and run."

Deputy Fred Johnson began, "CSI worked up the paint sample and has narrowed it down to Ford products from 1989 through 1997. It cannot pin down the make other than it was a Ford and could be one of several models. There has been no luck with any garages or body shops. No local bars report anyone too drunk to be driving in the late afternoon. All the known DUI's we talked to have alibis."

"Could have been an out of stater," Deputy BB Larkin said.

"What about salvage yards?" Deputy Susan Black asked. "Not a long stretch for someone to trash an older Ford, have it crushed."

"If it could have been someone from out of state, what about from Canada?" asked Deputy BB Larkin.

Deputy JC Cardozza added, "We are expanding our search to include the entire state and neighboring states. For sure I will consider the possibility that the driver could be Canadian. As far as salvage yards go, we did inform salvage yards and other police forces, even the state police. Everyone we talked to, we reminded them that Brooks has offered a fifty-thousand-dollar reward for information to the identity of the driver that killed his wife. Any other questions or comments?"

When the room was silent, Sheriff Cooper again talked to his deputies. "I'm getting pressure from the governor and the Westover mayor. The governor hinted at a state budget cut to the city and that would surely affect the sheriff's department. Two state senators called me and asked about the investigation. Appears that Brooks has a lot of friend throughout the state. If any of you read the New Progress this morning it devoted a half-page to the accident and our responsibility to Brooks and how the community owes him a lot for the legal work he has done for free for both the city and state."

There was a few of deputies murmuring among themselves when Deputy Al Smithson asked, "Any news on the state trooper shooting? Didn't see anything about it in the paper."

Sheriff Cooper answered him, "Nothing that I've heard or can report on."

"The original news said a light blue Ford. Is it possible the hit and run driver was fleeing the accident when the trooper tried to pull him over? In a panic, he shot the trooper?" Deputy Al Smithson asked.

Sheriff Cooper replied, "It is a remote possibility. According to her husband she normally ran late afternoons, before evening, and would return before dark and the trooper was shot near the end of his shift that ended at eleven. She was hit miles away from the shooting and the driver was going in the opposite direction maybe hours before the shooting. I'll run the possibility past them and see what they say. In the meantime, everyone knows what the accident means to us, let's get to it and solve it. I don't want to see my name or the sheriff department in the paper again."

Chapter 4

From his sheriff's deputy car, Deputy Two Trees could see girls playing soccer. He waited until they were finished and approached the group. Not knowing what they looked like he asked if anyone of them could point out the four girls he wished to talk to. As it turned out, the girl he approached was one of the four girls Carmen had named and her three companions were the other three. When they identified themselves, he called the four off to the side and began to question them. "This won't take long. Please be patient with me, I'm taking over for the other deputies and everything is new to me. I want you to tell me about Angelina Corilla. Did she meet you at the mall last Wednesday?"

"No. We told the other deputies that she didn't. I didn't know that she was supposed to," Candice said.

He questioned Christy Miller, "Did you pick her up on Wednesday to take her to the mall?"

"Like I told the other deputies yes, but she had me drop her off about a mile from her place near the gas station on Elm Street. That is all I know," was Christy's response.

"Did you see her go into the station?"

"No. I saw her walk toward it and that was it. Never told me how she was going to get home or if she was going to meet up with someone and I never asked."

"Is it possible that she ran away?" Deputy Two Trees asked.

"No," replied Bonita Escadillo. "No, she did not run away. She was not that kind of girl. She would have told us."

"Juan says your brother asked him to arrange a date with her. Did you know about it, help him?" Deputy Two Trees asked.

Bonita was a bit surprised with the question. "No," she replied. "I definitely advised her against it. He's in a gang, no good for her. All he wanted was one thing and then he would have dumped her."

"We all liked her," Candice said. "She was one of our group. I think we would have known if she was going to run away."

"How about you, can you add anything," he asked Brandy.

"She used to be more athletic. Started out with us and then just quit. Wouldn't say why. All she would do was watch," Brandy replied.

"Did she date anyone? Do drugs?" he asked.

"No," Candice said. "Her mother would not allow her to go out with a boy. Said she was too young. No drugs that we would have known about."

"How well did she get along with her parents? Did she listen to them?" Deputy Two Trees wanted to know.

"As far as I know she listened to her mother. She wouldn't date for a few years. I think they got along fine, except for the dating thing. She wanted to date. I know a lot of guys at school wanted to date her, but like I said, she would wait," replied Bonita.

Deputy Two Trees was taking notes as he talked to the girls when he asked Bonita, "Can you give me the names of the boys who wanted to date her? I'll want to talk to them." Bonita gave him half a dozen names and she told him which of them were classmates and which were older. "Could there have been anything between her and Juan?"

"No," she replied. "If there was I think she would have told us. As far as I know he never made moves on her. He is more interested in her sister, Carmen."

"Yeah, but I don't think that Carmen would give him the time of day," said Candice.

"Can't prove it or know anyone that might know for sure, but I believe Juan may be gay," added Bonita. This last remark elicited chuckles from the girls.

After they quieted down Deputy Two Trees continued, "Her parents believe that she has been kidnapped and did not run away. Is that possible?"

There wasn't an immediate response. Finally, Brandy said, "Maybe. Well, yes."

"Why do you say maybe. Did she say or do anything that would make you say that?" he asked.

"I don't know," replied Brandy. "I just don't believe that she ran away so maybe being kidnapped is the reason she is gone."

Deputy Two Trees had no more questions, so he thanked them and gave each his card and told them if they think of anything to call him. He watched them walk away as they talked among themselves.

He got the address of the Myrince family and drove there. Their house was similar to the Corilla's, new among others in a recently developed area. When he was invited in he was quickly made aware that there were two preschool kids making a racket and there were several toys scattered around. Mrs. Myrince was a little overweight but a shapely blonde. She invited him to sit in the living room while she tried to quiet the two kids. He told her he was investigating her babysitter's disappearance and asked her to tell him about Angelina.

"Yes, Angelina was our babysitter and did a good job of watching my kids. I think she did it twice, maybe three times." She interrupted her talking when she yelled, "Katie take your brother into the other room until I'm through talking to the nice policeman." Both watched Katie take her brother's hand and lead him out of the room. Deputy Two Trees thought that she was well behaved and listened to her mother.

He soon asked, "Did you have any problems with her?"

"None that I can remember. Problems like what?" Mrs. Myrince asked.

"Do you know if she ever had a boyfriend visit her?" he asked.

"No. My Katie is a blabber mouth and would have said something about someone else being here, especially if she did have a boyfriend. She's a little young for a boyfriend, wasn't she?"

"That's what I am trying to find out," he replied.

"I heard that she has disappeared. I'm sorry she will not be available to watch the kids anymore. She was good with them," Mrs. Myrince said.

Like with the girls playing soccer, he gave Mrs. Myrince his card and told her if she can think of anything about Angelina to give him a call.

Deputy Two Trees drove to *El Rancho* restaurant, found a parking space a block away and walked to the restaurant. Since it was in the afternoon the restaurant was not busy. He went to the service counter and told the server who he was looking for. The guy behind the counter pointed to a table near the rear of the restaurant and said, "That's them. Hope you are here to arrest them. Tired of them hanging out in here. They's bad for bisness."

When Deputy Two Trees looked to where the server pointed he saw three young men sitting at a booth. He hung his badge on his belt so that it could readily be seen and walked to them, stopped and his stare settled on one of them. He could see that he was holding a cup of something and he was missing the last two fingers on his right hand. He had to be Three Fingers Lopez that Juan told him about. Before he could say anything Three Fingers Lopez returned the stare and in a sarcastic voice asked, "So, what can we do for you, dep-u-tee?"

"Tell me about you and Angelina Corilla!" he said.

Three Fingers said, "Nothing to tell. Don't know who you're talking about."

"Heard you wanted to date her. Maybe you tried and she said no," Deputy Two Trees said.

Sure that the deputy knew about him, Three Fingers said, "Didn't happen. I think back on it, I might've asked her friend Juan to get her to go out with me. He wouldn't and I didn't try."

His eyes shifted to a second member of the group and Deputy Two Trees saw that he had a resemblance to Three Fingers. He guessed he was Three Finger's cousin. "What about you Ronny?"

"What about me? What?" Ronny replied. If he was surprised that the deputy knew his name he didn't show it.

"You and Angelina, that's what!" replied Deputy Two Trees.

"Why you asking the same questions those other two dudes asked? We already told them. Don't you guys talk to each other," Ronny asked in a sarcastic way. He was sure that the deputy knew about him as well as his cousin Three Fingers. He waited and finally got out, "Same. Juan said no and I didn't try. Juan was protective of both of them Corilla girls."

The third member of the group appeared to be smug, and Deputy Two Trees assumed he could be trouble. He looked directly at him and said his name as a question, "Hector?"

There wasn't an immediate answer and when he was about to ask Hector a second time, Hector said in a defiant voice, "None of your business!"

Deputy Two Trees decided to accuse him. "So, you're telling me you did date her. I guess I will need to talk to you."

Hector fired back at him, "I didn't say anything. What I said, it's none of your business!"

If Hector wanted to play tough, Deputy Two Trees could play tough also. "So, you are telling me you did date her and you are ashamed of it or you have something to hide."

"No to both!" replied Hector. "It's just none of your business. I got nothing to say to the law, understand!"

"I'm sure that all of you know she is missing, I want to find out what has happened to her, that's all. I want you to tell me what you know about her, you and her, and if it's nothing, tell me."

Again, Hector tried to come across as tough. "I got nothing to say to you law-man, nothing."

"I think I've been respectable to all of you. Why are you the only one to give me a hard time?" Deputy Two Trees asked.

With what appeared as a sneer on his face Hector replied, "I don't like you and have nothing to say to you."

"Maybe I take you to my place for questioning. What do you say to that?" There wasn't a response from Hector, so Deputy Two Trees pressed on. "I put you in a holding cell for a while, lose your paperwork for a couple of days. Then you will have something you don't like me about." He let what he said to sink in then he asked Hector, "Now, tell me about you and Angelina."

Hector was silent for a moment. "Yeah, I tried to date her. She said no. Juan said no. Even asked my sister to help, guess what she said?"

"No," replied Deputy Two Trees. "Now that wasn't so bad. Why are you trying to be such a hard ass? So, even though you all wanted to date her, none of you did or had anything to do with her, is that correct?" There was no response but a shaking of heads, yes. "Do any of you know if any of your friends did? Ask her out? Have trouble with her? I take your silence and shaking your heads no, means no?"

This time Hector spoke, "No. That's right. Know nothing else about her."

"Any of you three know of or hear of her being dated by someone other than one of your friends, someone over friendly with her?" He saw the three shake their heads no.

The three were silent. Not looking up at him Three Fingers mumbled, "I heard the mayor's son maybe took her out, he was seen with her. Just a rumor. Reason I wanted to take her out."

"Who told you that?"

"I don't remember, just heard it," and he was silent.

Ronny spoke up next, "That was why I wanted to date her. If she was going to begin dating, why not me? The mayor's son is white, she is not, and we are not. Maybe she should stick with her own kind."

"Yeah, that's right," Three Finger added.

Deputy Two Trees looked directly at Hector and asked, "What about you Hector?" He didn't respond. "That maybe she would go out with you. Hear you wanted only one thing from her, that true?" Hector looked away from the deputy and refused to respond.

Ronny answered for him. It sounded like he wanted to get onto the good side of the deputy. "Like he said, no. If he took her out he would have wanted to brag about it." Hector gave him an aggravated sneer.

"You are all a lot older than her; she was only thirteen. That didn't bother you?"

"As Hector used to say, if she's old enough to bleed, she's old enough to butcher," Ronny replied.

Deputy Two Trees was through talking to the three men and told them if they hear of anything that could possibly shed light on his investigation call him and he and he gave them each one of his cards. He got up to leave when Three Fingers said, "Goodbye, dep-u-tee. Come back and see us anytime."

Chapter 5

Deputy Two Trees was sitting at his desk as he looked at his notes and compared them to what Deputy Breem had written in his report. He read that Hector Escadillo had been antagonistic. He read that he believed Hector wanted to seem tough to his friends. He wondered what to do next, maybe a private talk with Carmen. Maybe as the missing girl's sister she could have heard something that he should follow up on, especially the rumor that Angelina had dated the mayor's son. What he wanted was for someone to say Angelina had dated the mayor's son, or at the least say he had been seen with her, not just a rumor. Then he would bring him in for questioning. There was nothing concerning that in Deputy Breem's report. He would follow up on him, but now he was wondering how he could get Carmen's telephone number since she wasn't listed in the phone book. Simplest and most direct approach would be to ask her parents, tell them he wished to speak to her alone.

His thoughts were interrupted by the department receptionist Ms. Lee. "Cory, a Miss Miller called and wants to talk to you. Wouldn't say what it was about. She sounded nervous and hesitant. She hung up before I could transfer her call to you. She said to meet her in the picnic area after the soft ball game this evening in the ballpark on the west side. And, oh yes, Mrs. Two Trees wants you to call her. She said her son never answers his phone messages."

"Thanks Linda. I'll take care of both," Deputy Two Trees answered her.

"Don't forget you are coming to my place this weekend for Ralph's barbecue," she continued. "I've invited a neighbor and her daughter also. She's a nice girl. The kids are looking forward to seeing you again and playing that card game you showed them."

"Linda, don't try to find a girlfriend for me," he replied.

Linda tried to defend herself. "It's not like that. I just wanted you to know who the strange woman was among all your friends."

"I know. Tell Ralph to make sure the beer is cold and tell your kids they better practice the card game, or I'll beat the as usual," Deputy Two Trees answered her.

It was not quite evening but late afternoon and Deputy Two Trees was in the park near the soft ball field. He sat on a picnic bench and could hear the game's onlookers cheering. He watched the game from a distance and after ten minutes he could see the fans leaving. The game was over. He saw Christy Miller approach. He invited her to sit at the table with him. "Did your team win?" He saw her shake her head no. "I remember that you didn't say much earlier when I talked to your friends. Do you know something that you want to tell me? That maybe you dropped her off on previous occasions and could add to what you said."

There wasn't an immediate answer. He waited. Finally, Christy said, "I don't know why I called you. I guess I just wanted someone to talk to about Angelina. There's nothing I can tell you that might be a help. Yes, I did drop her off at least two other times, but I don't know where she was going, who she was to meet. or how she was to get home."

"Please Christy, if you know anything, no matter how insignificant it may seem, it could be a help. By keeping it a secret, you are not helping her or her family," Deputy Two Trees told her.

He saw Christy look down at the wooden tabletop and with her fore finger trace the initials carved into the tabletop. He waited. She was struggling to tell him what she wished him to hear. He would allow her to decide on when to talk. She picked at the wood tabletop. "What those others told you was not exactly true," she eventually replied.

"What was not true?" he wanted to know.

"I know she went out with Michael Morrison several times," Christy said, and she looked away toward the ball field.

Deputy Two Trees was sure he heard her correctly. She had just verified what Juan's friends had said was a rumor. "You mean she went out with the mayor's son?"

Christy continued to look away when she answered, "Yes. She kept it quiet. No one else knows. I think she only told me. I think she was going to meet him when I dropped her off."

At first Deputy Two Trees was taken aback but he quickly recovered. "Why do you think that?" There wasn't an answer from Christy. "Is that it? What can you tell me about their dating? About him?"

"Nothing. She never talked about him, where they went or what they did. All I know is that she once remarked that he was very clumsy, not very mature. She never came right out and say that they dated. I never questioned her about her comments," Christy replied.

Deputy Two Trees could see Christy fidget. She knew more but didn't know how or if she should say anything more, so he waited. After a moment she began to say, "I probably shouldn't say anything because it was just a feeling I had, she never told me, but," and she hesitated and was quiet.

Deputy Two Trees waited for her to continue, finish what she had stared to say and finally asked, "But what? Never told you what?"

"I think she was pregnant," Christy almost whispered as if it would bite her if she said it out loud as she looked down to the ground apologizingly.

"What made you think that?" he wanted to know.

Christy didn't look up when she answered. "The way she acted and talked, quit soccer. I don't know if the others knew but she was throwing up a lot. Always told me it was something she ate. She once told me when he got those colored lights going, he was unstoppable."

"She ever tell you what that meant? Was she talking about Michael Morrison?" he wanted to know. "Could she have been referring to colored Christmas lights?"

Christy said, "I don't know. She never said. I never asked."

"What colored lights? Where could she have seen colored lights?"

"I don't know that either, what she meant," replied Christy. When I think back on it I'm not sure it was lights or light."

He had nothing more to add or ask about the colored lights or colored light. When he quickly ran through his mind where in the city there was any sort of colored light he came up blank, so after a moment of silence he said, "If I've heard you correctly, she and the son of the mayor of the city were sexually intimate?" Deputy Two Trees replied.

"What does sexually intimate mean? she asked.

"It means they were having sex," he told her.

"Maybe, she never told me that they were having sex," Christy said and then turned quiet. She had nothing more to add to their conversation. After some more prodding she said, "There's one last thing, she was attracted to older guys. Why she went out with Michael. He is several years older than she. That's it. There is nothing else."

Deputy Two trees knew she had his card and he reminded her if she thought of anything else to call him.

The next day he was in the outer reception area of the Ford and Corilla Real Estate main office. The receptionist told him she had contacted Carmen Corilla and she would be right out. Could she get him a coffee? No, he would wait for Carmen. After a moment, she entered the reception area and greeted him. When he had called her to make an appointment to see and talk to her she insisted he call her Carmen, not Miss. Corilla. "Come with me to my office Deputy Two Trees," she said. He followed her to an office that had her name on the door. Once he was inside she told him to sit across the desk from her and could she get him something to drink, coffee or a water. He declined both. Before he could ask her anything, she had to tell him about her work for her father. "After college, got my real estate license and I began working for my father and his partner, selling real estate and the occasional home. We were hoping that Angelina would one day also work here." She paused and waited for him to say something, when he didn't she asked, "Why did you want to talk to me here?"

Deputy Two Trees told her, "When your mother told me where you worked and gave me your telephone number, I told her, and now you, I want to talk to you alone, no interruptions by Juan. Maybe you can tell me something you wouldn't want your parents to hear. Sisters are often close and share secrets they would not tell anyone else. Angelina could have said something or hinted at that I should be made aware of."

"No. I told you everything I knew about her. There is a ten-year age difference between us as I told you, so we were not close in age. We spent very little time together. When I was home it was usually for dinner. I haven't lived at home since before college. I return home quite a lot but have my own place," Carmen said.

"Excuse me, but when I visited your parents and you were there, I just assumed you lived at home," he said to her. "The slightest thing that you may believe is not important can lead to something bigger. What was her relationship with Juan? He seemed quite concerned about her disappearance."

"Far as I know there was nothing between them. He is almost twice her age. I know he hinted that he wanted to go out with me. Asked me several times but I always believed a cover and that he was gay. Think he wanted to go out with me so that his friends wouldn't believe what I just told you. That is about all that I can say about me, him, and her," she replied.

"I have to ask, could she have been pregnant?"

"Absolutely no! She was only fourteen and didn't date! She was a virgin! How dare you ask such a thing!? I'm glad you came here so that Mom and Dad did not have to hear you ask!" Carmen said in an irate voice.

Deputy Two Trees knew as soon as he asked that it was a sensitive subject. "I'm sorry if I offended you, but I'm just covering all my bases. It is the reason a lot of young girls run away."

Still upset that the deputy had the nerve to suggest such a thing she quickly added, "Angelina was kidnapped! She absolutely was not pregnant and did not run away!"

He knew he was not going to get anything more from Carmen and he had upset her. If he continued to talk to her he was sure there would be a bit of animosity between them, so he got up, excused himself and decided to return to the office. He thought about what Christy had said about Michael Morrison.

Chapter 6

When he entered the department headquarters, he went to the sheriff's door and knocked. As soon as he was invited in he said, "Sheriff, I need to question Michael Morrison, the mayor's son. He wasn't mentioned in Deputy Breem's report, but his name came up twice as someone associated with my missing girl. I need your permission and I'd like a partner with me."

Sheriff Cooper wanted to know why, "Is he a suspect in the missing girl investigation?"

"I don't know. Right now, I only want to clear up some rumors I've heard about him, ask him a few questions," Deputy Two Trees replied.

"Okay, I'll talk to the mayor and get him to have his son come in voluntarily. Don't want to start people talking that he is being investigated for something unless there is strong evidence that he is involved. Walk lightly when you talk to him. Everyone is busy, especially with the hit and run case. Who would you like to partner with you?" asked the chief.

"I've worked with BB in the past and we got along well, how about him," was Deputy Two Trees' reply.

The sheriff didn't have to give it any thought when he said, "I'll arrange it."

Before Michael Morrison was to come in, Deputy Two Trees brought Deputy BB Larkin up to date on the investigation, what and why he wanted to talk to the mayor's son. It was the following morning in the interview room. Sitting at a table was Michael Morison, Deputies

Two Trees and BB Larkin. Deputy Two Trees asked, "Are you sure you don't want a lawyer, advise you of you of your rights, when to not say anything?"

"No. Why should I? I haven't done anything and was told that you wanted to talk to me. I'm not under arrest," Michael said.

"Just so you know we are videotaping our conversation," Deputy BB Larkin told him, "and you don't even know what we want to talk to you about?"

Michael was quiet, Deputy Two Trees said, "Tell us about you and Angelina."

"Who? You mean Angelina Corilla?" Both the deputies remained silent. "There is nothing to tell. I know who she is and that's about it," Michael replied.

"Didn't you date her?" Deputy Two Trees asked.

"No. All I know about her is who she is, and I heard she is missing," Michael replied.

"We have a witness who said you went out with her. Our witness says you more than know her," Deputy Two Trees said to Michael.

The look on his face said it all. "You mean that Angelina. We didn't date. I saw her a couple of times and that was it," he answered.

"Our witness said that you were quite passionate with her. You were more than just seeing her. Who am I supposed to believe? You or our witness?" Deputy Two Trees wanted to know.

"How old are you?" Deputy BB Larkin asked. After a moment of hesitation Michael mumbled he was twenty-two. "Well, Michael, she was thirteen, just turned fourteen and that means statuary rape." He let what he said sink in before he added, "That means you will get one year for every one of hers. Could mean you'll be thirty-five before you get out." He never said prison, but the implication was clear.

They could see that their suspect was taken aback and the threat was real. "Do you know where she is!?" Deputy Two Trees wanted to know.

"Okay, Okay. I might have dated her, but that was it. We would meet at that burger joint at the mall, have something to eat and then I'd drive her home. That's it. I don't know where she is. We never had sex! I swear. I'll take a lie detector test," Michael said.

"Tell us about the two of you," Deputy Two Trees said in a softer, we believe you voice. "But before you do, tell us about your colored lights."

"What colored lights? You mean Christmas lights?" Then he was silent.

There was a look of total puzzlement on the young man's face. It seemed obvious to Deputy Two Trees colored lights was a complete mystery to Michael. After a moment when it appeared Michael knew nothing about colored lights, Deputy Two Trees said, "Let's get back to you dating her."

Michael seemed to gather himself and said, "I saw her a few times, in secret. All we did was make out. I kissed her and felt her up. That was all. She wouldn't let me go any further."

"But you tried," Deputy BB Larkin said. Michael was showing signs of nervousness and he was about to press on.

"Yes, I tried. It's only natural. I think she expected me to try. This may not mean much, even though we didn't have sex, she was experienced," Michael said.

"What made you think that?" Deputy BB Larkin asked.

"It was the way she acted, things she said and where she would touch me. She would rub me through my pants until, until you know," Michael continued. "She knew how to get my motor running and then pull the plug. I knew that she had had sex with someone, but not with me. Take my word for it. Then one night she said she would not see me again, and she didn't."

Through with their questions they thanked Michael for coming in and let him go. They returned to the investigating deputy's office.

Chapter 7

Detective Two Trees could see his telephone light blinking. He picked it up and said hello. He heard Linda Lee say he has a phone call and she connected him to the caller. Deputy Two Trees immediately recognized the voice on the telephone. He heard his mother say, "I wanted to let you know that your cousin Sitting Calf had a baby boy."

All he could say was, "That's great news, mom."

"When are you going to come home for a visit Cory? You can bring Alice with you. Seems like forever since I've seen the two of you," he heard her say.

He knew he was not going to get away from his mother, so he decided to listen to her. "Mom, Alice and I are not together. I told you that weeks ago that we've separated and she's seeing someone else."

He heard her immediate response and knew that she did know about him and Alice and that they had separated, "You can come alone. I want you to meet someone." And there it was, come home and meet someone. He knew that his mother was aware that he and Alice had broken up.

He as quickly returned his mother's suggestion, "Mom, I don't want you to find a girl for me, I'll find my own."

She responded, "When? You're almost thirty. You always said you wanted a family and a dog. It's getting late for you."

He knew he would not win the discussion with his mother; he never has. "Mom, can we drop it? I'm not almost thirty, I'm only twenty-eight, and I have a new girlfriend."

His mother sounded excited when she heard the news. "You do? That sounds great. Who is she? What's her name?"

"She's just a girl. You wouldn't know her," he answered. There was a moment of silence. His mother was waiting for more information. When it did not come, he said, "Her name is Carmen." Before she could ask more questions, he tried to get his mother to stop talking about his love life and asked, "How is everything at the clinic?"

His ploy didn't work. "It's fine. Tell me about her," his mother said.

"Like I said, she's just a girl," he replied.

"When will I get to meet her," Mrs. Two Trees asked.

"Mom, would you quit pressuring me about her. Can we change the subject?" Cory asked.

His mother got off the woman in his life and said, "Tell me about the crime wave in Westover I heard about."

"It's not a crime wave. A state trooper was shot and killed, and a prominent lawyer's wife was killed in a hit and run. They are not related. As far as I know neither are going anywhere. Neither has a suspect and there are no leads."

As soon as he told his mother about the two cases, his mother asked, "Which one are you working on? Is he the lawyer you had trouble within the past?" Before he could answer her, she followed up with, "Tell me about Carmen." She had not forgotten about Carmen, who he had said was his new girlfriend.

"I'll tell you about her later. I'm working on neither," Cory said. "I've been assigned to a missing fourteen-year-old girl, we assume is a run-away. She may have been or maybe not be pregnant. Her parents insist that she was kidnapped. There has been a ransom request and they haven't heard from her for over a week and a half. I've put out a state-wide alert, nothing."

Mrs. Two Trees said, "The pregnancy opens up possibilities to investigate. Maybe taken out of state for an abortion or she is just hiding out with the guy. Any men in the area unaccounted for? Is she pretty?"

"Very," he replied. Then he stopped and had to ask, "Who are you talking about?"

"Carmen, who else?" she had to ask.

Again, he tried to steer his mother away from his love life. "You think just like dad."

"When you are married to a policeman, some of him rubs off on you. I'd like to meet her." Cory knew who she was referring to, he didn't have to ask. He was not going to be able to stop his mother asking about Carmen. "She could have been taken for sexual reasons, have you thought about that?"

"Maybe, but I don't think so. When the time is right," he could be just as evasive.

"There is always a reason. Things don't just happen. There is a reason and it may not be the most obvious. Why did she disappear? Same for the trooper and the hit and run. They may not in any way be connected but they just didn't happen, in the wrong place at the wrong time," Mrs. Two Trees said into the telephone.

"That is what dad used to say," he heard himself say. He was hoping that his mother had gotten off his non-existent girlfriend.

His mother was silent for a moment before she said, "There is another possibility, she has been murdered."

His mother was correct, but he answered her, "I thought of that but dismissed it. I liked the family and didn't want to assume that she may have been killed and didn't bring it up as a possibility."

"Well, I've got to get back to work. Good luck son. Hope to see you and Carmen soon. Call occasionally. Goodbye." Cory heard his mother say.

"Bye mom. I will," and he hung up.

As soon as he did his new partner said, "I didn't know you were dating anyone. Is she the sister of our missing girl?"

He looked at his partner Deputy BB Larkin and replied, "I'm not dating her and yes, she is the sister of our missing girl. It was the first name that popped into my head. It made mom happy and I hope will keep her as well as Mrs. Lee off my back."

"Yeah. I saw her pushing her neighbor's daughter on you at her barbecue. Apparently, it didn't work," Deputy BB Larkin said.

"No. It didn't."

Chapter 8

Monday morning when he came to work Deputy Two Trees saw two new men sharing a desk in the investigating deputy room. "What's going on Linda? Has something happened? Who are the new guys?"

Linda looked up from her desk and said, "Brooks convinced the mayor to allow private investigators he hired to work with us in locating the hit and run driver."

Deputy Two Trees shook his head in disbelief. "They'll just get in the way."

"Other than that, out at Sandy Creek a guy shot his live-in girlfriend. A fight broke out at the park, sent two deputies to the hospital. Suppose you will hear about both at this morning's briefing. A Mrs. Collins, fishing at the lake, said her dog brought something to her that she thought was a fetus. I sent a deputy to talk to the woman. He investigated it, thought it was a pig fetus, but to be safe he brought it in to the ME. Guess what Cory?"

"It was human," he replied.

"Give that man a cigar. The ME wants it investigated," Linda Lee said and then switched subjects. "What do you think about Darlene? She is pretty, isn't she? Will you give her a call? I'm sure she would like to hear from you. Her mother thinks you are wonderful."

"Linda, you're as bad as my mother, don't try to fix me up with anyone. No, I don't intend to call her. I'll find my own girlfriend, thank you," was his response.

Later that morning after roll call Sheriff Cooper called to Deputy Two Trees. "Cory., come into my office." He entered and the sheriff indicated that he should sit. "What progress are you making on the missing girl?"

"Not much so far. Have a few hunches that I hope to follow up on and that is about it. Nothing to report. Maybe Breem's decision to call her a run-away was correct," Deputy Two Trees replied.

"Until you have something solid, stay away from the mayor's son. I don't want him threatening me, shouting how my deputies brow beat his son," the sheriff said.

"We just asked him a few questions and that was all. You can watch the video. BB may have suggested he could be in trouble, but that was it. He is the only real connection we have that the missing girl was involved with anyone," Deputy Two Trees replied.

The sheriff's response was, "Do what you have to, but be careful. I do not want our minority community saying that our office did not pursue their case with vigor." Deputy Two Trees believed the conversation was finished when the sheriff added, "Since you seem to be getting nowhere, we are short-handed, especially with the hit and run, take BB with you and talk to Laura Benner, the ME about the fetus brought in. I know that the two of you can't split your time between the two cases, but you will have to. See if either of you can make progress on the fetus case or BB can work it and you can stay with the missing girl."

Deputy Two Trees knew that the sheriff was serious and that the conversation was finished. He would not be able to come up with a valid objection to the sheriff's additional assignment, so he mumbled an, "Okay." Sheriff Cooper dismissed him.

Deputies Two Trees went to the detective room told BB Larkin what the sheriff had said and the two headed for the ME. They talked a little about the extra load they may have with the dead fetus, but both knew that for some reason it seemed that quite a bit of crime was going on. Even several deputies were pulled off routine traffic patrol and speeding enforcement and had been assigned to crimes. When the two reached the morgue, they entered. "What can you tell us Ms. Benner?" Deputy BB Larkin asked the ME.

"It is human," the ME said, "about five, five and a half months old, dead for well over a week. I believe that it had been buried and was not the result of the dog dragging it. The woman would have begun showing she was pregnant."

Deputy BB Larkin asked, "Could it have been natural, maybe a late miscarriage and discarded?"

The ME's answer was, "As MacDuff says, untimely ripped from my mother's womb. But unlike MacDuff, this fetus did not survive."

"Who is MacDuff?" Deputy BB Larkin asked.

Lura Benner said, "Never mind. The fetus was cut out of the woman and then probably buried. There would have been a lot of blood."

"Someone's idea of a home abortion?" Deputy Two Trees asked.

"Maybe," the ME said. "Done by an inexperienced person. There were cuts on it."

"Possibly by the dog, maybe bites?" asked Deputy BB Larkin.

"No'" she replied.

"So, we need to begin looking for a woman who may have been hospitalized, about a week or so ago," the deputy again said.

They could see the ME shaking her head no. "Look for a woman that is dead. I believe it could not have been removed without killing her. Bring me suspects and I will be able to tell you for sure who the father and the mother were. I can show you the remains but doubt you will be able to see that it was human. Here are several photos." She handed three pictures to the deputies. She was correct, they couldn't identify it as a dead fetus. "Good luck deputies. Keep me posted."

They thanked the ME and left the morgue. Deputy BB Larkin was the first to speak, "Guess we should start to look for women in the area who are missing."

"I only know of one for sure, Angelina Corilla, my missing girl," Deputy Two Trees said.

"You start with her," Deputy BB Larkin said, "I'll check for others."

It was later that day when Deputy Two Trees called Carmen Corilla and asked if he could meet with her. She informed him that she often eats lunch at a small restaurant around the corner from her office, she could meet him there. "That would be fine, but first I want to apologize for upsetting you at our last meeting, I would prefer that we meet somewhere private, maybe your office again?" Carmen declined but said she would go home for lunch and meet him at her apartment and gave him her address and said she would be expecting him at noon.

When he arrived at her apartment he was invited in. He saw it was small and tastefully decorated. She had stopped at a deli on the way home and had bought two sandwiches for them to eat. She busied herself making him a cup of coffee. He sat and waited for her. When she sat, he ran over in his mind how he was going to approach what needed to be said and what he had to ask her. He watched her take a bite of her sandwich, he only looked at his. He couldn't put it off. He would talk non-stop before she could respond. "Please don't be offended about what I am about to tell you. If you are. I apologize to you beforehand. Miss. Corilla, we have found a dead fetus. The mother was most likely killed. I know you don't want to hear this, but the only woman missing in the area that I readily know of is your sister, Angelina."

"No! No! It can't be her," she said. "She was a good girl, couldn't have been pregnant. You're mistaken!"

"I hope that I am wrong, but I must follow up on all possible leads related to this case." He waited for Miss. Corilla to settle down before he continued. "If I could get a sample of her DNA, I can quickly find out one way or the other. I need something that you know has been in her mouth."

"When she would read, she would chew on plastic straws and save them in a bed side table drawer. I told her it was disgusting but she wouldn't stop. I'll go to mom and dad's place and get you one," Carmen said in a more controlled voice. Deputy Two Trees believed that she possibly accepted the fact that her sister had been possibly killed, or believed and hoped beyond hope, that it wasn't her sister. She would help him prove it was not Angelina's.

He said, "I'll drive you."

She was totally under self-control when she said, "Not until after you finish your lunch."

It was later in the day when Deputy Two Trees told Deputy BB Larkin that he had taken a sample of the missing girl's DNA to the crime lab. "I gave the lab a straw my missing girl had chewed on and the DNA is being analyzed. We should get an answer in a day or two."

Deputy BB Larkin said, "I've found two women in the area who have been reported missing within the last two weeks. One left only a week ago after a big fight with her mother but has called and wants to come home. The second disappeared during the correct time frame but I was told by her sister she ran off with her boyfriend. A friend of the boy's said they ran off to Vegas to get married. I'll follow up on her, make sure it is true and I'll look for others."

Their receptionist Linda Lee told the two that the sheriff would like a word with them. When they walked into his Sheriff Cooper's office Deputy BB Larkin asked, "How are the new guys doing?"

Sheriff Cooper replied, "Don't ask. Lucky you two don't have to work with them. Brooks has upped the reward for info concerning the death of his wife, a hundred thousand dollars now. He has gone on TV seeking any information concerning the car or driver. The place is swamped with calls. We can't possibly check out all of them."

"Send those private dicks to check them out," Deputy BB Larkin said.

"I have," the sheriff replied. "Anything form you two? I've got two deputies beaten at the park. They both were checked out at the hospital, released, but both were advised to stay home and take it easy for at least a week. I'd really like a little bit of good news from anyone. I read your report to date Cory, one of the guys in the fight we have in a cell, you talked to him, Hector Escadillo."

"Don't believe he had anything to do with the missing girl and he wasn't too cooperative. Maybe now he can point me in a direction I know nothing about," Deputy Two Trees said. "Think I'll pay him a visit. We are at a standstill on both of our cases, but we hope something will break. I still think that Brooks should be a suspect and questioned. All the stuff he is doing might be a way to deflect suspicion."

Sheriff Cooper said, "Forget about him Cory. Unless we come up with something that could possibly tie him to the hit and run, we stay clear. Especially you."

When Deputy Two Trees saw Hector Escadillo, he was as uncooperative as before and this time more belligerent. "Well mister tough guy, what do you have to say?"

There was no response from Hector, only a glare from the man in the holding cell. "If you can help me with Angelina I can possibly talk to the arresting officers and maybe, just maybe, have the severity of your arrest lessened."

There was no response from Hector. "I know nothing, I got nothing."

When he got back to his desk Linda had a message for him. He should contact the morgue. CSI had analyzed the straw's DNA and the ME Laura Benner, wanted to see him. He went to the morgue and talked to the ME. When he returned to his desk his partner was there. "I just returned from the ME. She had the report on the straw's DNA and compared it to the fetus. A perfect match."

"So now we are going to be looking for someone who was screwing a thirteen old. Don't think that will narrow the field any," Deputy BB Larkin said. "To start, I think we should talk to Michael Morrison again. Let's call him in."

"Maybe you're right BB, but the sheriff told me to be very careful talking to the mayor's son, take it easy on him. We should have a compelling reason to talk to him," Deputy Two Trees said.

"If it wasn't him, he could possibly point us in the right direction we keep talking to him, mention something the girl could have said to him,"

Deputy BB Larkin replied. "I'll talk to the sheriff, tell him what and why we want to talk to the kid again."

"Before we do, I want to talk to the woman who found the fetus and look over the area. The sheriff said he sent a CSI team to search the area soon as the fetus was identified as human. After two hours or more, they found nothing. What the dog found could have come from anywhere. They searched an area about three hundred feet from where the woman was, saw nothing that looked like freshly dug by the dog. I also have to talk to the Corilla family concerning what we found, they are definitely not going want to hear what I have to say," Deputy Two Trees replied.

Deputy BB Larkin told his partner, "I'll go to the lake with you but let you go alone to talk to the family."

They got clear instructions from Deputy Larry Cummins of where to find the woman and drove there. It was the shore of Elmwood Lake in a wooded area. The lake had an irregular shoreline so the area they were in was secluded, a small inlet in the shoreline and not visible from a large part of the lake. Near the lake was a small camper with a boat trailer attached to it. The camper was connected to the rear of a pickup truck. Near the camper and below a canvas tarp that was held up with two aluminum poles was a small table and several folding aluminum lawn chairs. The two deputies parked near the camper and got out. A short distance from the camper was a woman, back to them, standing in front of a painting easel. When the woman heard their car pull in she placed her paints and brushes on a small wooden table that was near her, reached down and picked up her small dog, a Yorkshire Terrier. The two approached her and identified themselves.

"This is where you are fishing Mrs. Collins?" Deputy Two Trees asked.

She smiled at him when she said, "Yes. Not many fish this side of the lake. Water's too shallow and now that it is almost summer, the water is too warm. Not much plant life because of the sandy bottom that you can see that comes up onto the shore and into the woods. It may be true or not, it's what my husband tells me."

At her answer, Deputy BB Larkin had to ask, "Then why fish here?"

"It gets me out of the house, it's not crowded, a nice view that I can paint with no interruptions. The dog can run free, and mainly, I don't have to clean any fish. You can see that I don't have a fishing pole. Husband's in a boat out there somewhere and I make him clean what he catches. My part is, I will cook them and eat them," she replied.

"I like your painting of the lake and it's far shoreline. Only a small area of the shore but nicely framed by the trees on either side. How long have you been here?" Deputy Two Trees asked.

She smiled at the deputy for the compliment before she answered, "Four days. We'll leave tomorrow, maybe this evening. All depends on whether my husband is lucky today. We have about a half dozen fish in the camper's freezer. That's enough. You know, I told all this to the other deputies who were here. They pissed off my husband, said they were scaring away the fish," Mrs. Collins said. "What a laugh, scarring away the fish."

"We are new so you will have to excuse us if we ask the same questions. Can you tell us about the incidence?" Deputy BB Larkin said.

"My little Elsie here," and she stopped and patted her dog, "was running around in the woods." She stopped talking to the deputies and now talked to the dog. "Weren't you my little pumpkin?" She turned her attention to the deputies and continued to tell what had happened, "I called Elsie and she came to me with the thing in her mouth. Didn't you sweetheart?" She looked at the dog as though she expected an answer.

Deputy Two Trees asked, "Where do you think she was running around?"

"All over I think. See that big tree over there," and she pointed to a large tree maybe thirty yards from the lake.. When she seemed satisfied that the deputies looked at the tree she referred to, she continued, "That was the last time I saw her and when I called her, she came around that tree with the thing in her mouth. At first I thought it was a dead squirrel."

Deputy Two Trees thanked her and said to his partner that he wanted to look around. They could see evidence of many footprints made by the CSI team when they began to search beyond the tree. They walked back and forth and soon the lake was out of sight. Deputy BB Larkin said, "Lot of sand mixed with dirt and a lot of brush. Would have been easy to bury something and difficult to find. Anything, or anyone, buried would not have a tell-tale burial sign."

Deputy Two Trees agreed and continued to walk and look. After several minutes, he came across a second dirt road. "I wonder where it goes to?"

Deputy BB Larkin looked in the direction the road went and said, "My guess it goes to the lake. I don't know if you noticed, but when we talked to Mrs. Collins, if you looked to the right, a couple of hundred yards along the shore a huge rock formation comes down to the water. You couldn't see beyond it. This road leads to the water beyond the rock. I have to believe that it's used by fishermen."

"She said there weren't many fish this side of the lake, water was too shallow," Deputy Two Trees replied.

"Yeah," Deputy BB Larkin uttered, "but maybe the water is higher beyond the rock and in the spring."

"This is the spring," Deputy Two Trees replied.

"Well, it could very well be used by young lovers." They were quiet and turned back to where they had parked. "There is nothing to say that it couldn't have been brought here by boat," Deputy BB Larkin said as they walked back.

"I remember what the ME said, there would have been a lot of blood. If this is my missing girl, transporting a bloody girl to a boat could attract attention," Deputy Two Trees answered. "Could be he did put her in a boat, but tie a concrete block to her and it, dump both in the lake."

BB answered him, "If he intended to dump her in the lake, why the abortion?"

"Thinking that way, she would not surface," Deputy Two Trees said.

"The fetus could have come free of a rope, surface and wash to shore," his partner replied and then added, lake's too big to drag." They were both quiet for a moment before he said, "A better scenario would be that she and it, were driven to this area on either of these two roads."

Deputy Two Trees thought about all the things his partner had brought up and was quiet for a while. He eventually said, "Maybe you're right. I'm going to check out both dirt roads for a couple of nights. See if young lovers may have seen something that I should know about."

"Not me," Deputy BB Larkin replied. "You are really stretching now. It will be a waste of time. Have someone from the night shift do it."

When he returned to the station, Deputy Two Trees called Carmen Corilla. "I know you are at work, but I would like to talk to you, alone, either your office or your apartment or you can come here to the station."

There was a moment of silence. Did the deputy want to talk to her about her sister, ask more questions, or like before, not be interrupted by Juan? A last remote possibility was that he was attracted to her and wished to spend time with her. She answered, "I'll quit work early this afternoon. I'll be home and will be expecting you to come by at three o'clock."

He thanked her and hung up. Cory Two Trees was not looking forward to telling her about her sister. But giving families bad news was part of his job. He and Deputy BB Larkin arrived at her apartment about ten minutes until three and parked. He no sooner parked his car when Carmen pulled in. She walked to him and asked, "What do you want to see me about?"

"Not here in the parking lot, let's go inside," was his reply. He followed her inside and up to her apartment. His partner stayed in the car. Once inside he told her to sit and he began. "I'm sorry that I have to tell you this, but the dead fetus we found was that of your sister's, Angelina."

"No! No!" Carmen said and she stood up and confronted the deputy. "It's impossible! She couldn't have been pregnant." After a moment, she came to the realization that maybe it was true and she asked, "How can you be sure!? Maybe you made a mistake!"

"Our medical examiner and crime lab are positive. DNA doesn't lie. I'm sorry," He repeated. He saw her clinch her fists, bite her lip and shake her head no. Her eyes began to mist over, she was about to cry but she turned away from him. He could hear her stifle a silent sob. When he believed that she had time to take in what he had said and come to grips with it, he took several steps to her and put his hands on her shoulders.

Without turning to face him she uttered, "It means she is dead?"

Deputy Two Trees had to tell her the truth, "I'm afraid so." She leaned her head to the side and put her cheek on his hand. He could feel a tear drop fall on it. He waited. She straightened up and went into another room and returned with a Kleenex, wiped her eyes and blew her nose. "I have to break the news to your parents; you should be there." She shook her head yes. "I'll drive you."

"Mom will have trouble accepting this, that my baby sister was pregnant and is now dead," Carmen said. "They will have to believe you."

Chapter 9

That night Deputy Two Trees drove down the dirt road to where he talked to the woman camper. The camper and truck were gone. He wondered if her husband had a good or bad day on the water. Which would cause them to want to leave? Her husband caught more fish, or he didn't catch any. He drove back out to the paved road and watched on his left side for the second dirt road that he and his partner had come across. He drove close to a quarter mile before he spotted it and turned to enter it. He drove over a half a mile before he could see the partial moon reflected off the lake in front of him. The road ran down to the water so that fishermen could back their boat trailer to the water and unload their boat. To his right the road had a large turn-around area and was partially hidden by trees. He saw nothing or no one that he could talk to. Both areas near the lake would make for good lover lanes. Tomorrow night, both areas would again be checked. Deputy Two Trees pulled into the turn-around area and turned around. When he was headed back in the direction of the dirt road he saw his car lights reflect off something. He continued to turn around so that his car was headed back in the direction he came down the dirt road. He stopped, turned on the car's police flashing lights, grabbed his flashlight and headed toward what he thought was a reflection. It was a car. He shined the flashlight onto the car's license plate, thought that he could remember it, shined his light into the car and knocked on the roof. He shined the flashlight on himself so that he could be seen as a deputy. "I am Deputy Cory Two Trees. I want to talk to you. Get dressed."

The man in the car asked as he pulled up his pants, "What's the problem? We're not in a public place."

"When you two are dressed, walk to my car." He walked off toward his car, opened the door and got in. He ran the plates and saw that they showed the car registered to a Carl Best. He saw the two lovers walk to his car. He reached over to the back seat and opened the rear door and told them to get in the back seat and he turned off his interior lights. As soon as they were seated he said, "What are your names?"

As he assumed, the man's name was Carl Best. The woman said, "My name is Denver Drews, but everyone calls me Denny. Are we under arrest?"

"No, I'm not interested in what you were doing. Want you to answer a few questions, how often do you come here?"

Denny was able and seemed anxious to answer him, "Once in a while, maybe a couple of times a week. Why?"

"If we are not under arrest, what's this all about? Did my wife send you?" Carl Best asked.

"I'll ask the questions, you answer them, okay?" He waited a moment before he continued, "You're cheating on your wife?"

Carl Best defended himself as best he could, "Yeah, so what, she's never home. Works nights and is always tired. I have needs."

When she heard Carl's answer, Denny spoke up, "You said you loved me, your wife doesn't understand you! Is that a lie?"

"Denny, I do love you!" Carl answered her.

"And we will be together as soon as your divorce is final?" Denny replied to her boyfriend's remark.

"Yes," Carl said. "I didn't say exactly when."

"You did! As soon as you were divorced!" she told him, and Deputy Two Trees saw her slide away from him on the rear seat.

"The two of you shut up!" They both fell silent. "I didn't see a side road; how did you get your car there?" Deputy Two Trees wanted to know.

Carl Best decided to tell him, "We like it private so I drive to the shoreline and drive along it a ways and turn off to where you found us."

"Why hide so well?" Deputy Two Trees asked.

"He said he didn't want anyone to see us at my place, his place or a motel, that's what he told me," Denny replied.

"Did you ever see anything unusual around here?" he asked the couple.

"Like what?" Denny asked.

"Anything during the last two weeks? Maybe other lovers here acting funny?" he again asked.

"No," Carl replied. "Quite a few cars have showed up but nothing unusual."

"What about that couple?" she asked Carl.

"It wasn't unusual," he replied.

"You don't see it every day is all I'm saying," Denny told him.

Deputy Two Trees interrupted their bickering, "Tell me. Let me decide."

"It was no big deal," Carl said. "They were skinny dipping, so what."

"Are you going to tell me or not?" the deputy asked.

Carl Best began, "We were parked where you found us, just talking when this car comes down the road and parks in the turnaround area. A couple who wanted some privacy."

"We weren't just talking!" Denny had to say. "Then a second car comes down the road, maybe ten, fifteen minutes later. It stops right at the water's edge. They leave the lights on and get out of the car. They strip off their clothes and run into the lake."

"In a few minutes they come out," Carl added.

"They start to make out," she said.

"Yeah, first thing you know he has her bent over the hood of the car and is doing her from behind. They didn't know that we were watching," said Carl.

"But they knew the other car saw them," Denny added.

"How did you know about the other car?" asked Deputy Two Trees.

"If you were to ask me I'd say he was showing off. Strutted around showing how hard he was. Tuned sideways to the other car so they could clearly see him," uttered Denny,

"Carl, is that right what Denny just said?"

"I don't know. He could have," was all that Carl said.

"That's because you were focused on the woman. You couldn't see anything except her big tits and that she was blonde," Denny accused her boyfriend.

"They finished, got dressed and left," Carl said. "Several minutes later the other car left too."

"Yeah, thought the two cars were together. That's why he was strutting around in front of the other car, showing off to who was in it," Denny added.

"Can either of you tell me anything about either of the cars?" He could see them shaking their heads no.

"It was dark," added Denny. "I think I may have seen the guy somewhere before, but I'm not sure. He was in and out of the car's lights, so I asked Carl what was on his left arm. I thought it was a big bruise."

Carl replied, "It was a tattoo. Couldn't see what it was. It was dark and both cars were dark."

When Deputy Two Trees was satisfied with what the couple could tell him he offered to walk them back to their car. He heard nothing that could add any information to the fetus found in the area. He didn't say anything about their cheating, it was no concern of his. The way they seemed to squabble he believed they were headed for a rocky marriage if Carl did get a divorce and they married. He watched their car drive along the beach and then leave. He stayed for an hour and a half but saw no new parkers. Maybe the spot wasn't as popular as Carl and Denny believed.

The next morning Deputy Two Trees was talking to his partner, Deputy BB Larkin. "Should have been there. Caught a couple doing the nasty. The only thing they had seen since they apparently parked there often during the past two weeks, was another couple doing the same.

I'm not giving up though. I intend to check it out again, especially this weekend."

"Don't look at me that way. Before you say anything, I'm not interested in going with you Cory, so don't ask," Deputy BB Larkin told him.

They were interrupted by Sheriff Cooper. "BB, you and Cory come into my office."

The two deputies entered the sheriff's office and waited to find out what the sheriff wanted. Deputy BB Larkin asked, "What's up sheriff?"

"I'm getting a lot of heat from the mayor on the hit and run. Most likely he is being pressured by Brooks. I don't want to, but BB, I'm taking you off the missing girl and the fetus, putting you back on the hit and run. Fred needs help running down all the leads he has been getting."

When he heard this, Deputy Two Trees complained, "Sheriff, I need help. I need BB."

"Sorry Cory. I've even pulled some of the guys from night shift to help. Okaying over-time," Sheriff Cooper said. "Had to. When I got a call from the governor's office asking if we were getting any closer to solving the case, didn't take a genius to get the message. Cory, you're on your own again. BB, go see Fred."

Chapter 10

Disappointed with the news, Deputy Two Trees returned to his desk. His phone rang and he answered the call. "What is it Linda?"

He heard the sheriff's department receptionist say, "Cory, Denny called. She left a number and wants you to call her. Should I be concerned about the two of you? She sounded kind-of-sexy on the phone. Is she as pretty as Darlene?"

He wondered why Linda was so concerned about his love life. She wasn't so nosy about other single Deputies. He would have to disregard any comments she made or make up a non-existent girlfriend. "Linda, she is a possible witness to my missing girl."

"Didn't sound like a witness to me," he heard Linda say.

He dialed the number Linda had given him and he recognized Denver's voice as soon as she said hello. "Miss. Drews, this is Deputy Cory Two Trees. What do you want to talk to me about?"

"Call me Denny," she said. "I remember something else about that night. Can you come by my place this evening after I get off work?"

He didn't wish to see her at night when he asked, "Can't you tell me now?"

"No. I'm at work and we are not allowed to make personal phone calls. I called you on my break." She said she would see him around seven and she gave him her address.

Deputy Two Trees spent most of the day following up on classmates that might have known Angelina and got nowhere. That evening at seven thirty he rang the buzzer of Denver's apartment. When she invited him in he saw a small apartment. It was not well furnished, and he could see that even though she had tried to tidy the place up, it was still messy. In a word, the place was tacky. In the full light of the apartment, he could see she was sort of pretty, a dark-haired woman, but needed help in dressing and putting on makeup. He got right to the reason he was there. "You have something to add to what you saw? Tell me."

"Yes. I do," but before she told him anything she changed the subject. She reached down, grabbed hold of the light sweater she wore and lifted it up to reveal her breasts. She thrust them toward Deputy Two Trees and asked, "Do you think my tits are too small? Carl thinks so. Hinted at maybe I could get a breast job, an enlargement."

Slightly taken aback Deputy Two Trees stayed in control of the situation and said to her, "Miss. Drews, pull your top down. I am here on official business!"

She made no attempt to do what he asked. She looked at him then down at her breasts and then up. "They may not be large, but they are real. Do you want to touch them?" and she cupped one in her hand. Cory looked her in the eye. The disdain on his face told her no. "Carl says he is waiting to divorce his wife, should I believe him? Do you think I should wait or look around?"

"Miss. Drews, please! If you don't have anything to tell me, I'm leaving."

"Okay," and she pulled her top down to cover her breasts. "I never said, but I'm a waitress at the Eat-n-Go. A lot of times deputies and state troopers stop in and eat. That's what I wanted to tell you. Remember, I thought that I'd seen the guy before at the lake. He was a state trooper. I had seen him in the restaurant."

"Are you sure Miss. Drews?" deputy Two Trees asked. He thought to himself, so what. The trooper could not have had anything to do with his missing girl.

Denver interrupted his thoughts when she asked, "I'm pretty sure. Do you want a drink?"

"I'm here as a deputy on the sheriff's department business. I'm positive. Maybe some other time," he said to her.

"If you ever change your mind, give me a call." She saw him shake his head no and added, "I don't know what you're investigating, but whatever it is, I want to be kept out of it. You involve me I'll say I never told you that."

"I'll do my best Miss. Drews," he said and left.

Chapter 11

S taking out the two roads that went to the lake that weekend proved fruitless. On Monday morning, Deputy Two Trees was in the sheriff's office with the sheriff. "I know it is not my case and I shouldn't be investigating it, but if what my witness told me was true, the guy she saw skinny dipping at the lake was trooper Jake Cooke. She was sure that he recognized the other car parked there and maybe the passengers. Maybe someone important, prominent, having an affair. It would be a stretch, but it is possible he was shot over that."

"Had to be random. Today someone having an affair would go to a motel, not park near the lake like a couple of teenagers."

"I caught a guy running around on his wife with his girlfriend at the lake. I don't think it would be out of the question," was Deputy Two Trees response.

"How could the shooter possibly know where Jake would be that night?" the sheriff asked.

"He wouldn't. I stumbled across it and am passing it on to you. You go to the state police with it is up to you. I checked with the ME and she told me Jake did have a large tattoo on his left arm, just like my witness claimed she saw. If need be I can have a second witness verify it," Deputy Two Trees said to the sheriff.

Sheriff Cooper said, "I'll run it past the state police and let them decide whether to follow up on it or not."

"My witness is having an affair with a married man and would like to be kept out of this if possible. I told her I'd try," Deputy Two Trees said to the sheriff.

"I won't mention who the witness is. I'll try not to involve her. And the Corilla girl?" he asked. "Is there anything to make the family feel better?" the sheriff wanted to know.

"Nothing. They know that she had been pregnant and is now dead. The mother broke down when I told her, wanted to deny it. Cried and cried, left her with her husband and daughter to calm her down. I don't think there is any way to make them feel good except to find their daughter's killer and see him brought to justice," was Deputy Two Trees' response. "Since the investigation is stalled, does the department have enough money for me to bring in a cadaver dog? I'd like to search the area where the fetus was found. If it were buried it wouldn't be a stretch to believe the Corilla girl is buried there too."

Deputy Two trees could see the sheriff thinking about what he asked for. After a moment, the sheriff said, "I'll look into this year's budget and get back to you."

That afternoon Deputy BB Larson was talking to Deputy Two Trees. "They found the hit and run vehicle. A couple of fishermen spotted it in deep water off the rocky ledge in Elmwood Lake."

"That is good news. What does CSI know about it?" Deputy Two Trees asked.

"For right now all they know for sure is who it belongs to. It had stolen plates, but the car belonged to a guy who died couple of years ago, and his eighty-tree year old widow doesn't drive. CSI is going over it right now. They will find something. You have any luck, any lovers over the weekend?" Deputy BB Larkin asked.

"No to both. Tomorrow I'm to meet with a cadaver dog and its handler. Going to take them out to where the fetus was found. I told the sheriff if it was buried, why not the girl too?' Deputy Two Trees replied. "A cadaver dog could be a big help."

Sheriff Cooper walked through the investigator room and stopped at Deputy Two Trees. "Cory, the state police are not interested in whether the trooper was or was not having an affair. Seems that he was known as a lady's man, had flings with a lot of women and believed he was living with a woman when he was shot. They are looking at the possibility that his current girlfriend could have a jealous ex-boyfriend or maybe some of the other women in his life had boyfriends who had it in for Jake. I was told they are getting nowhere."

After the sheriff turned and was about to leave, Deputy BB Larson said, "Had to be a random act, how else could it be explained?"

Over his shoulder the sheriff got the last word in, "He stopped someone who did not want to be stopped, the guy who stole the car. Maybe they will find something in the car they found that could point their investigation in the right direction."

That night Deputy Two Trees decided to take home the information that he had and look for anything that could tie anything together. He pulled into the parking lot over-flow area. When he would leave, he would back up and hopefully hit a curb in the parking area before he would run onto a lawn of about twenty feet. Beyond the lawn was a tree and brush area that had not been developed when his apartment was built. Unseen by him was a man thirty yards inside the trees. He was dressed in black and was holding a rifle with a telescopic sight. It rested in the 'Y' of a small tree, its butt against the man's shoulder. Prior to Deputy Two Trees parking the department cruiser, the man had been looking through the telescope's sight as he moved it across the windows of the apartment building. He would switch from watching the apartment windows and focused on cars that pulled into the parking lot. When Deputy Two Trees pulled into the parking lot, the man stopped moving the gun and found the deputy in the rifle's telescopic sights.

Deputy Two Trees turned off the car's engine. He reached for the files he brought home and one slipped out of his hand and fell to the cruiser's floor. He bent forward to retrieve the file. In the moment that he did, the man with the rifle squeezed the trigger. The bullet struck the driver side window and it shattered. Glass flew into the vehicle cutting Deputy Two Trees on the left side of his face. He didn't know exactly what had happened but knew that he had been shot at. He stayed bent over and pulled himself across the seat to the other side of the car. He grabbed his car's microphone and at the same time opened the passenger side door. He just was about to slide out of the car when a second shot hit the driver side door and fragments of the bullet flew over his head. On the ground, he called into his microphone who he was and that he was in the Fairview parking lot and that he was under fire. He requested any cars in the area to respond. He held onto the microphone and drew his service pistol. He stayed crouched down and crept to the front of his cruiser. He lifted his head enough to look over the top of his car. When he did, he heard a third shot smash into the cruiser, a fourth one went wild. He stayed down and waited. What could he do, a pistol against a rifle? Before he could pursue a course of action he heard the siren of a deputy's cruiser and then he could see the flashing lights. The deputy pulled close to his cruiser, stopped, and jumped out and joined Deputy Two Trees. Both deputies aimed their pistols in the direction of the woods, and they peered over the car's hood. No shots followed as two additional deputy sheriff's deputies pulled into the parking lot.

The next morning in the roll-call room Sheriff Cooper was addressing his deputies. "For those of you who didn't hear, Deputy Cory Two Trees was shot at last night and almost killed. Someone hid outside his apartment and shot at him four times with a high-powered rifle. CSI found where the shooter waited and found three spent 7mm magnum cartridges. They were clean, no fingerprints. Captain Myers of the state police called and thinks we need to look at cases where there were very outspoken and upset perps or their families who may still be holding a grudge against law enforcement officers. They are looking into their cases and instance where their men were involved as witnesses or arresting officers."

"Why so?" asked Deputy Susan Black.

"Cory is working on a missing girl and not much in his past that was threatening enough to warrant this sort of a response. And Jake Cooke, all he did was basically catch and arrest speeders, no arrests for anything that caused him to go into court," the sheriff said. "So, in the past week or so a state trooper was killed and now an attempt on one of my deputies."

Deputy JC Cardozza said, "Both were trouble free, right sheriff? No reason to kill either unless," and he paused, "unless someone has a desire to kill lawmen."

"Don't be so fast to judge," Deputy BB Larkin said. "There was that incident between Cory and Brooks. I heard it was pretty heated."

"That was between him and me. I seriously doubt the guy he was defending was involved and I doubt Brooks wasn't that upset he'd want to kill me over it." Deputy Two Trees replied.

Deputy Al Light said, "But Brooks' client was sent to prison, right Cory?"

"And he's still there," was Deputy Two Trees' response.

Sheriff Cooper interrupted the murmuring among his deputies. "I've assigned several deputies to escort several of our judges who have presided over big cases. In the meantime, everyone always wears a vest. Sergeant, this includes both patrolmen as well as investigators."

After roll call was over Vern Smithson followed Cory Two Trees to his desk and sat across from him. "Cory, the sheriff assigned me to investigate your shooting. Bring me up to date on what you are working on."

Deputy Two Trees answered him, "I can handle it myself."

"Maybe so. But I want you to tell me where you are in your investigation, who you talked to, maybe upset," Sergeant Smithson said to him.

Deputy Two Trees looked at Vern and shook his head in disbelief. "Vern, I'm searching for a missing fourteen-year-old girl, Angelina Corilla. None of the people I've talked to were upset and most tried to help me."

"Any of them not happy with the questions, the progress you are making?" the sergeant wanted to know.

He thought about his investigation to this point. "Maybe three could have shown concern. Juan-Hernando Medina, a friend of the Corilla family wanted more progress finding the girl. Then there was Hector Escadillo. Could have been involved, but I doubt it. He wanted to date the girl. Acted tough, belligerent. More of an occasion to sound tough with his friends. I've checked on him and he is awaiting trial for an altercation with a couple of our department who tried to break up a fight at the ball field. He's still in a cell. Then there is the mayor's son, Michael. He had dated the girl, but they broke up. If anyone was upset with my questioning him, it was his father the mayor."

"Anything else come to mind?" Sergeant Smithson could see his fellow deputy Cory shaking his head no. "A big case you were involved with?" Again, he could see him shaking his head no.

"The only big thing I was involved in was the drug dealer Brooks was defending. My testimony sent him to prison. Brooks' client got fifteen years but with good behavior will be out in less than ten."

"Going back a few years, what about the family of the guy you shot?" Sergeant Smithson asked.

"From what I could tell at the time, the entire family was happy that he was out of their life," Deputy Two Trees replied.

"He have any close buddies, maybe wanted to get even with you?" was the next question asked by the sergeant.

"The only one I was able to find was the guy he shot and killed," Deputy Two Trees replied. When he thought about his past he could not think of anything serious enough that someone would want to kill him over.

"How about a jealous boyfriend? Are you seeing anyone?" he was asked.

"No," Deputy Two Trees replied. "I am not seeing anyone and me and Alice separated over two months ago."

All the while Sergeant Smithson took notes. When he believed that there was nothing else for Cory to add, he said, "You heard the sheriff. A 7mm magnum. He meant business. Make sure you are wearing a vest."

"Don't know if it would stop such a bullet, maybe slow it down," Deputy Two Trees replied.

"Wear one anyway," the sergeant said. "If you think of anything else, let me know."

After his talk with Sergeant Smithson, he called Carmen Corilla. He asked her, "What is your relationship with Juan?"

There was a moment of silence before he heard her say, "Just friends. His father and my father are friends. He's like a brother. He's closest to my father. Why do you ask?"

"Is it possible he could be upset with the lack of progress I've been making, upset enough to do something drastic?" He heard her say no when he asked, "Could he be jealous of me?". While he waited for an answer he picked at the edge of one of the two band-aids on his face.

"I don't see why," the deputy heard. "I've never given him a reason to believe that there is anything between us other than you are investigating Angelina's disappearance. I've never been that close to him, especially romantically and as I've said I think he may be gay. I've not given him any reason to be jealous of you and why would he?"

Deputy Two Trees continued his questions of her. "Was there ever anything between him and Angelina? He wouldn't want her to be found?"

He could feel Carmen thinking about what he asked. "No. Like I said Deputy Two Trees, he was like a big brother and treated her like a sister. I would have to say he looked after her."

"To be sure, could you get me a sample of something he has had his mouth on, a cup, or a soda can. Just so that I can eliminate him."

"Yes, I'll try. Is that all?"

"Yes, no. You don't have to call me Deputy Two Trees. Call me Cory," and he hung up. He wondered why he didn't tell her there was an attempt on his life last night and he had no good reason not to have told her.

Hector Escadillo was still in jail for his involvement with the two deputies in the park. He crossed him off the list of possibilities. That left the third possible assailant that he told Sergeant Smithson about, Michael Morrison. When he thought about the mayor's son, he felt it very improbable it could have been him who tried to kill him. But, on the other hand if he did kill Angelina, he could be that desperate. What about his father? Could he know about his son and Angelina and tried to protect his son? He decided that a second interview with the mayor's son was necessary.

Chapter 12

Deputy Two Trees got out of the SUV. A prominent sign on both sides of the vehicle said it held a police dog. He walked to the rear of the SUV with Deputy Oldhouse who opened the rear window, and he pulled the bottom half down to open the rear of the SUV. He then reached into the rear to the dog cage, opened its door and clipped a leash to the dog's collar. He called to the dog and she jumped onto the ground.

Deputy Two Trees asked, "What's the reason for the hunter orange vest?"

The dog handler, Deputy Kevin Oldhouse, answered, "So I can see her if she's loose and it will protect her chest if she is running through the brush."

Satisfied with the answer, he next asked, "What's her name?"

"Savannah. You shouldn't try to pet her. She has a job to do and needs to focus on it. Where should we start the search?"

Deputy Two Trees pointed to the large tree and said, "That is the tree that the woman fishing indicated was the first place she saw her dog with the fetus. She had no idea where the dog had found it. CSI coverer about a hundred yards or so and found nothing, no dead girl or a hole that the dog may have dug."

"Come on Savannah," he said and walked to the tree.

The two deputies walked back and forth with the dog in an ever-increasing arc for an hour, and like the CSI team, found nothing. Deputy Two Trees though it was a good idea, but it was a long shot and now he realized it proved fruitless. Deputy Oldhouse stopped, and Deputy Two

Trees asked, "Are we going to call it quits?" Deputy Oldhouse didn't say anything but knelt beside the dog and took hold of its collar. He was a bit surprised when he saw Deputy Oldhouse unclip the leash and let the dog run free. "Is that a good idea?"

He heard the dog's handler say, "We've walked over this area for over an hour and found nothing. I'm letting her run free. She can cover a lot more ground than us walking with her."

"Is that safe?" Deputy Two Trees asked as he saw the dog bound off. "Is it a good idea? Could she get lost?"

"Hopefully, she will get a whiff of decaying flesh and zero in on it. She'll return when I blow my whistle," Deputy Oldhouse replied.

As they talked, he could see Savannah crisscross and she quickly covered a lot more ground. She was soon out of sight and he thought that they were close to the second road to the lake where he saw Carl and Denver. "I don't see her. Could she be lost?" he asked Deputy Oldhouse. He couldn't hear anything, but he could see Deputy Oldhouse blowing a silent whistle.

After a moment, Deputy Oldhouse said, "She should have returned. Let's look for her over there, the last area I saw her," and he began to walk to their left.

They didn't walk far before they spotted the orange of her vest. Deputy Two Trees said, "There she is, lying down in that pile of brush. I see her vest." As they got nearer to her Deputy Two Trees was sure she was whining. "She could be hurt!"

"No. She's pawing the ground, trying to scrape away some of the brush. Help me move some of this crap," Deputy Oldhouse said and he reclipped the leash back to the dog's collar. When the area was clear, Savannah went to it and laid down. When he saw this, he said, "She's found something." He picked up a dead tree branch and the deputy began to dig in the area.

"Whoa! Whoa!" Deputy Two Trees said. "We have to call CSI, let them look."

Deputy Oldhouse stopped and looked at Deputy Two Trees. "You want to get a CSI team out here to dig up a dead squirrel?"

Deputy Two Trees heard what the dog handler said, and he agreed. "You're right. It will be easy to dig through this dirt and sand. Let's find out." He broke off a dead tree branch and helped dig and remove sand and dirt with his hands. Savannah lay at the side and watched them dig. When he glanced at the dog, Deputy Two Trees could see that the dog looked mournful.

They hadn't dug for more than a minute when Deputy Oldhouse uttered, "Uh-oh."

Deputy Two Trees asked, "What is it?"

He heard from his digging partner, "We better call CSI. This is a blanket and if I'm not mistaken, this is a foot."

An hour later an area of maybe fifty feet was cordoned off around the body with yellow police tape. A hundred yards away on the dirt road deputy cars and the morgue vehicle could be seen through the trees with their lights flashing. After a videographer filmed the area from different angles, a CSI tech and a man from the ME's department went to the body and began to uncover it, all the while their work was taped. When the blanket was cleaned off, the CSI tech and the man from the ME's department exposed the body of a young woman. As best that they could, the body was cleaned of sand and dirt and they began to examine it. Finished, they had two deputies help lift the body out of the shallow grave by lifting the blanket. They placed both the body and blanket in a body bag and with the man from the ME's department, would begin the trek to the coroner's van. Two deputies were scraping away more of the sand that had covered the body and carefully searched it. Other deputies were searching the area and looked for anything that could be tied to the body. All total there were ten people at the scene. The CSI tech went to Deputy Two Trees and invited him over to look at the body. They unzipped the bag to expose the girl. When he looked down at it he saw what he thought was a young woman, nude from the waist down, her stomach cut open revealed part of her internal organs. "Deputy, is this your missing girl?"

Deputy Two Trees said, "I believe so, but I'm not positive. Maybe I see her in the morgue cleaned up I'll have a more positive answer."

The CSI technician replied, "We did the best we could under the circumstances. The body has disfigured having been in the ground for several weeks. If I had to guess I'd say for sure the cut open stomach was a clumsy abortion and most likely killed her."

It was the next day and Deputy Two Trees was told by the sheriff that there now was a definite murder victim and BB Larkin had been re-assigned to work with him. The two walked to the ME's office and Deputy Two Trees said, "Only person that I know had anything to do with her was the mayor's son, Michael. We definitely need to talk to him."

"Remember the sheriff said to go slow. Doesn't want the mayor calling him again," Deputy BB Larkin replied.

They entered the morgue, saw the ME, Laura Brenner, and walked to her. "I got a message that you wanted to talk to me," said Deputy Two Trees.

"I've got your girl on the table," she pointed to a covered body on an autopsy table.

All three walked to the covered body and the ME pulled the sheet down to the girl's ankles. He noticed now that she had been cleaned up, even though she may have been in the ground for almost two weeks and her flesh had begun to deteriorate, she must have been quite attractive. Her stomach had been sewed together by the ME. Deputy Two Trees heard the ME ask, "Is this your missing girl?"

He looked more closely at the face of the dead girl and slowly shook his head up and down. "Yes, it's her."

"What can you tell us about her?" Deputy BB Larkin asked.

"She's about fourteen or fifteen. She was pregnant and the clumsy abortion I sewed up. Like I told you before, there would have been a lot of blood even though she was dead," the ME said.

"What do you mean already dead?" asked deputy BB Larkin.

"The guys at the scene assumed the cut open stomach was the cause of death, it wasn't. After I examined her, the cause of death was strangulation. One of her neck vertebrae was broken. I have the x-ray if you want to see it. The cut-out fetus was done after she was dead. Whoever did this was a strong man and I believe didn't want to do it. You remember the tentative cuts I told you about on the fetus?" The two deputies didn't answer but she could see them shaking their heads yes. "Well, I found several tentative cuts on her stomach too. He cared for her. Not any blood found at the scene because he cleaned her off before burying her. Explained the cuts, he didn't want to do it, didn't want to cut her."

"Why perform the abortion if she was already dead?" asked Deputy Two Trees.

"When you catch the guy, you can ask him. My guess he wanted to see it, what it would have been if allowed to live. His child," Ms. Brenner replied. "Then buried it later. Why the dog found it. Most likely you wouldn't have. CSI searched around where the body had been buried and found no evidence that it had been near her. Not in the same place as the body because my guess is the guy did it at night, couldn't find exactly where he buried her. Like I said, you can ask him when you catch him, but he cared for the girl and his unborn child, wanted them to be together."

"That road is a lover's spot. Wouldn't he be taking a chance returning to the scene? Deputy Two Trees asked.

His partner Deputy BB Larkin replied, "Most likely checked the area out first for others and did it early in the morning, before it got light out, small chance others would be there then. Lovers wouldn't stay all night and too early for fishermen."

That afternoon Deputy Two Trees had parked in front of the Corilla house. He was not looking forward to what he must tell them. There wasn't the possibility that he had made a mistake, their daughter was dead, he found her body. He had called Carmen and asked her if she could meet him at her parent's home. He rang the buzzer and was invited in.

As soon as he entered he heard Juan before he saw him, "Well, look who's here? If it ain't the law. What do you want l-aa-w man?"

Deputy Two Trees answered Juan using a firm voice, "This doesn't concern you. I want to talk to the Corilla family alone." He could see Carmen give Juan a stern look and he moved away from Mr. Corilla, into another room. When Juan was out of the room, the deputy told them, "Mr. and Mrs. Corilla, I believe that I have found your daughter's body."

"No! No!" she cried. "It can't be my Angelina!" Mrs. Corilla said, and she began to cry and her husband put his arms around her and held her.

At the sound of Mrs. Corilla crying Juan came back into the room. "What's going on in here!?"

Ignoring Juan, Mr. Corilla asked, "Are you sure it is her?"

Before he could reply Carmen took her mother's arm and told her to sit down and then sat beside her on the sofa. Without looking at him she told Juan, "They have found Angelina's body."

Juan looked at Deputy Two Trees and asked, "You're positive!?"

Deputy Two Trees replied not only to Juan but included the entire family, "I am certain. The ME is checking her DNA against the straw Carmen gave me and will know for sure in a day or two. I am sorry. Someone from the family will have to come to the morgue and make a positive identification."

There wasn't an immediate response when Juan said, "I'll do it."

"Thank you, Juan, but it must be a family member," Deputy Two Trees told Juan.

Carmen replied to the deputy, "Mom, you and dad can stay home. I'll do it. Juan can you stay with them?"

"No," Juan said. "I'll drive you Carmen."

Deputy Two Trees said, "No, I'll drive her."

At the morgue, Deputy Two Trees showed what the CSI techs had gathered. "Yes, I gave her that blouse last Christmas and I'm sure this is her charm bracelet." She picked up a gold chain necklace and said she didn't recognize it and put it down.

She looked at Deputy Two Trees. He asked her, "Are you ready?" his hand on her shoulder he turned her in the same direction of the viewing window, its Venetian blinds closed.

"I don't know if I can do it," she replied.

"If you would like, I can show you a picture and you can make an identification from that?" Deputy Two Trees told her. He tried to make the identification less confrontational for her. He could see her shake her head no. She straightened up and took a deep breath. "Here, take my hand," and he held hers. "I'll signal them to open the blind," and he touched a button and spoke into a microphone at the side of the window. He could feel her squeeze his hand as she readied to look.

The Venetian blinds opened, and he heard her gasp, then a silent, "Yes, it is her." She turned away from the viewing window, so she was now facing him. He saw her eyes begin to mist over; she was going to cry. "Hold me," she said. Deputy Two Trees put both arms around her and held her close to him. She stifled a sob when she asked, "And she had been pregnant?"

"Yes. She had been," he replied. He could feel and hear in Carmen's voice that she was now in control of her emotions.

"How could someone do this to a person? He must at one time felt something for her. How could he stand hearing her scream?" were Carmen's responses.

Deputy Two Trees whispered into her ear, "She didn't feel it, the ME said she had been strangled first."

Still in disbelief Carmen asked, "How could this have happened?"

"Come I'll drive you home."

When they reached Carmen's parents place she was about to get out of Deputy Two Tree's police car when she opened her purse and took a Coke can from it. She held it on its bottom and handed it to Deputy Two Trees. "Here, something that will have Juan's saliva on it."

Angelina's body was released that afternoon and when Deputy Two Trees checked with the funeral parlor who was to do the burial, he found out that the viewing would be a one-day event. Most likely because of the disfigurement of the girl's face. The make-up artist of the funeral parlor did a decent job of making her look presentable. He planned on going to the burial and see if anyone stood out of place. He was not sure of standing out of place meant, but he would attend the funeral. He saw quite a few people at the internment and as his gaze move around the group, none stood out as out of place. It would prove to be fruitless and after the interment, Carmen approached him, took his hand, and thanked him for showing up.

Chapter 13

It was morning and the sheriff was at the podium addressing his deputies in the roll call room. "For those of you that haven't heard, Cory has found the body of his missing girl and now he and BB are investigating a murder as well as the possible murder of a fetus. The car pulled from the lake is the hit and run vehicle. A piece of Connie Brookfield's clothing was caught in the headlight chrome. No license plates were on it and the state police believe that it could be the vehicle involved in their shooting. They are continuing to investigate the car. Fred and JC will bring you up to date." He handed the meeting over to the two investigating deputies.

Deputy JC Cardozza stepped up to the podium. "A light blue 1991 Ford Taurus was the car we found. CSI found some clothes in the trunk with a name written on them, Mary Jennings, a retired eighty-three-year-old schoolteacher. Also found were some pencils, several 12 gauge shot gun shells and a spent .45 caliber casing. No prints. Mary's husband had been a hunting enthusiast, explained the shot gun shells but not the .45 casing. Her husband had never owned a pistol. It could definitely tie the car to the trooper shooting. Our CSI are going over everything a second time with the state police."

Deputy Fred Johnston continued their investigation to date. "After her husband died, the car had been parked in her garage and not driven for the last several years. She didn't know that it was missing. The plates on it that Trooper Cooke checked were stolen from a different car. Its owner and his wife had been on a vacation in England. Could have been stolen anytime during the previous week. The shooter removed the license plates before he drove the car into the lake. He didn't know that the trooper had already checked on their validity. Here's the kicker, Brooks Brookfield's fingerprints were found on the car's driver's door. Turns out that Brooks recently went over Mary's will with her and one of the items in the will was the car. He said he touched it when he talked to her about it. Wanted to see if possibly it had value."

"Plus," Deputy JC Cardozza interjected, "he had a million-dollar life insurance policy on his wife. If he did kill his wife, why would he shoot the trooper? He has no motive and has no record of ever having a .45 caliber pistol. But, as a defense attorney would know people that could get him one and there would be no record of it."

"We should have listened more to Cory and looked at him as a possible suspect. Maybe could have saved some time," Deputy Fred Johnston told the gathered officers.

He then handed the meeting over to the sheriff, Frank Cooper who told the gathered deputies, "Brooks has been arrested for the hit and run of his wife. The DA wants more evidence that the hit and run was murder. I want everyone to keep digging I want to make the DA happy."

Deputy Two Trees spoke up, "I guess Brooks is going to need a good lawyer." At this statement, there was general laughter among his fellow deputies.

The coke can Carmen provided Deputy Corry Two Trees proved that Juan was not involved with Angelina and was not the father of the fetus. Later in the day Michael Morrison and his attorney, Lawrence Kowalski, were sitting at the table in the interview room. Most of the questions asked by Deputy Two Trees were similar to the ones he originally asked and were answered by Michael. Deputy BB Larkin said, "Michael, we are now looking for the murderer of Angelina Corilla. We know you were the only guy that had contact with her."

"We can clear this up with a DNA sample," added Deputy Two Trees.

As soon as Deputy Two Trees suggested the DNA sample, his lawyer said, "No. He will not, and there will be no questions without me being present. He said that he answered all your questions during his first interview. If there is nothing new. We are leaving." Attorney Kowalski stood up.

Before he could turn to leave and before Michael stood up, Deputy Two Trees said, "We hear you work out. You're pretty strong, aren't you?"

Michael's lawyer said, "Don't say anything." He looked at Deputy Two Trees and said, "You want to know anything you ask me, and I'll decide if he should answer or not. What could his strength have to do with any of this? Unless the murdered girl was killed some way by a strong person."

"No. No. Just an observation," Deputy Two Trees replied.

"Well, don't observe anymore without talking to me," Attorney Kowalski said.

"You're awfully touchy about this," said deputy BB Larkin. "He got something to hide, be guilty about?"

Attorney Kowalski sat after the last remark. Deputy Two Trees asked, "If he didn't do it, have anything to do with the death of Angelina, why not give a DNA sample?"

Without saying no, Michael's attorney said, "If you don't have anything else, we are leaving." He got up and at the same time put his hand under Michael's elbow to indicate that he should also rise. The meeting with the two deputies was over.

When they were at the door Deputy BB Larkin said, "We will be in touch."

Attorney Kowalski said. "That's fine. You have my number you want to talk to him again."

The two deputies returned to the investigator's room and sat at their desks. Deputy Two Trees was the first to speak, "Her family said she baby sat several times a week and gave me the dates that she would have done it. But after a second interview with Mrs. Myrince, she told me she only ever did it twice. I checked and on several times when she was supposed to be babysitting but wasn't, the Morrison kid had rock solid alibis. I also checked with her friend Christy who picked her up several times and then dropped her off. She didn't know where Angelina went or who she saw, how she got home. Whoever she met up with, they were apparently very careful and did some planning so they wouldn't be seen."

"Where and what was she doing on those occasions? The big question is, who was she meeting," Deputy BB Larkin replied. "You said that Myrince and Christy could add nothing. How about her sister Carmen? Sisters often share secrets."

"She was my first one to question, but she only saw her occasionally when she went home for a dinner mostly on Sundays. They lived separate lives for the last ten years or so," Deputy Two Trees replied.

"We know how and why she was killed. Now we must find out who," Deputy BB Larkin said.

"Do we know why? Was it because she was pregnant or was there another reason?" Deputy Two Trees asked.

"The fetus could have been cut out as if to say, I told you to do," Deputy BB Larkin said.

"Maybe so, but it takes us back to the big question, who?" Deputy Two Trees replied. "Could it be someone important and having sex with a thirteen-year-old girl could ruin a career, a marriage, send a guy to jail? Could the scene that Denver described to me be connected? Who was the woman with Jake? Who was in the other car that Denver said he was showing off to?"

"Does it matter? How could what they saw have anything to do with our dead girl, and a dark car at night?" Deputy BB Larkin asked.

"At least we have a witness who can identify the woman with Jake at the lake, if we can find her," Deputy Two Trees replied. "I'm going to try and find her, if I do, maybe she can tell me something about the other car or its occupants."

"A better idea, let's check the areas that our girl was let off by Christy. Maybe someone saw her meet a guy, get in a car. A better possibility than a strange blonde and a dark car at night that are in no way connected to her," was Deputy BB Larkin's response.

The remainder of the day was spent by the two deputies canvassing the two areas Christy had told Deputy Two Trees about. One area was a strip mall and the second was near a filling station. They showed Angelina's picture and knocked on a lot of doors, both shops and residences, no one remembered seeing her. If they had seen a woman, it was night, and they could not swear it was her.

Chapter 14

Deputy Two Trees didn't give up on his idea of identifying the woman skinny dipper at the lake. He was in the parking lot of a local lighting fixture store, 'Billy's Lights for the Home', where Carl Best worked as a salesman. He had called him and arranged to meet after he got off work. Cory waited for Carl and when he approached the deputy's car, Deputy Two Trees invited him into his car. He began to talk about that night, "Can you remember anything else about that night? Forget the woman. I'm interested in the other car. Besides being dark, its make or model? Big? Little? Anything?"

Carl Best thought back to the night and was silent. Finally, he said, "Nothing. I don't remember if the car was big or small. What did Denver tell you?"

"Pretty much the same," was deputy Two Trees' answer.

"What did you tell my manager was the reason you wanted to talk to me? Wasn't about me and Denver, was it?" Carl wanted to know.

"No. I told him you may have witnessed an accident and I needed to talk to you about it, nothing about you and Denver," was Deputy Two Trees' response.

When Carl was about to leave, he stopped with his hand on the door handle. "I think I've seen her before, the blonde."

"Where? When?" asked Deputy Two Trees.

"I can't remember. She just seems familiar," replied Carl.

"If you can remember anything else about her or the car, call me," and Deputy Two Trees gave him another card.

For the remainder of the day, he and Deputy BB Larkin talked to anyone that Angelina may have known and talked to. They tracked down fellow school mates, teachers, mall employees where she bought her clothes. The gold necklace was real gold and expensive but could have been bought anywhere. No one in the family could remember when they first saw Angelina wear it. Her family just accepted it as hers and never talked about it or asked where she got it. There were at least a dozen stores in Westover that sold this necklace and none of the salespeople remembered the girl in the photograph they were shown, nor could the two deputies give them an approximate time that the necklace would have been purchased. Was it sold to any men they could remember? The answer was yes. It seemed at least a half dozen men had purchased the necklace. None could be traced or identified. The same was true for the three pawn shops they visited. For the second day, their search turned up no one who could shed any light on Angelina or someone she may have dated. They counted back the months she was believed to be pregnant. Who she was seen with, talked to? Cory interviewed her friends again, could they remember anyone four or five months ago she may have mentioned in passing. Not necessarily someone she dated, a boy's name that may have come up in conversation. The only name that came up was the mayor's son, Michael. They didn't know that they had dated, but she talked about him occasionally. Christy again was singled out and questioned alone with the same questions. She repeated that Angelina had gone out with the mayor's son. Did she believe that Angelina had been still seeing him or any guy? She did not know, would have to say no, and could add nothing to what she originally told him. Did she know about the necklace? Where it may have come from? No, but Angelina had mentioned that they were on sale at the mall but did not say definitely that was where she got it.

That night when he got to his apartment, Cory Two Trees drove to the far side of his parking lot and parked the sheriff's deputy car assigned to him. It was further from his apartment building, but it was not directly in line with the trees. When Cory pulled into a parking space and got out, he paid no attention to a car he heard start. The car he heard start began to move toward him. Lights out, he didn't see it before he could hear it. Halfway across the parking lot the car approaching him speeded up and raced straight at him. When he realized that the car was going to hit him, he dove to the side as the car sped past him. He got up, gun now in hand, he saw the car speed around the corner of the parking lot, tires squealing and drive out of sight. It happened so fast he didn't see the license plate or the car model except it was big and dark. He believed it was an older Chevy. He returned to his car and started to race after the car.

Once out of the area, he didn't know which direction the car had gone. He decided on a street and sped down it. After ten minutes, he knew he had chosen the wrong street, so he drove back to his apartment. The car could now be anywhere. He called for help but could not describe the errant car except to say it was big and dark, maybe an older Chevy, and most likely would be speeding.

The following morning, Cory was in the sheriff's office explaining what had happened the night before. "Cory, someone is out to get you," the sheriff said. "This is someone not with a grudge against the sheriff's department, but you in particular. Have you looked closely at your past cases, someone holding a grudge against you?"

"That was my first thought, but after the shooting at me, I did look and could find nothing that stood out," he answered the sheriff.

"Have you ruffled any feathers talking to people about your dead girl?" Sheriff Cooper asked.

"No," he replied. "I do know the mayor's kid, Michael, and his lawyer were upset. According to you the mayor himself is also unhappy about me questioning him. I don't think either would be that desperate to try and kill me, even if the kid did kill the girl. I can't tell you anything about the car except I thought it to be an older Chevy, no license plate. It was dark and I was diving for my life."

"I'm assigning you to desk duty until we can clear this up. Deputy Vern Smithson will be investigating the attempts on your life," Sheriff Cooper said.

"Frank, you can't do that! I've got this case, the dead girl to work on!" Cory said to the sheriff.

"Well. It can and will. I can't afford to lose you," the sheriff replied.

Deputy Two Trees would not give up on working on his case. "BB is my partner and I'll stay close to him. He can pick me up in the morning and drop me off at night and I promise, I will not work at night."

The Sheriff listened to Deputy Two Trees plea and said, "Okay, but if another attempt is made on your life, it will not be discussed, you will be on desk. Is that clear?"

Later that morning the sheriff talked to Deputy Cory Two Trees. "I hope Deputy Smithson made it clear."

"Yes. BB is going to stick with me like glue," Deputy Two Trees said with satisfaction. "Where are the private detectives?" he asked.

Sheriff Cooper smiled when he answered, "Gone. When Brooks was arrested, there was no one to pay them. You never did bring me up to date on your dead girl."

"Both BB and I think that the Morrison kid is involved, but he went quiet when his lawyer told him to shut up," Deputy Two Trees replied.

"The mayor has distanced himself from Brooks after he was arrested and is looking to protect his son. You and BB continue to pressure the son," Sheriff Cooper said. "I know you don't think so, but is it possible that the son, or his father the mayor, could be behind the attempts on your life? Deputy Smithson is going to look at them, start poking around."

"I doubt it. I don't think either of them have the nerve," Cory replied. "But BB and I are going to continue checking on the son's whereabouts on the nights the dead girl was supposed to be babysitting."

Sitting at his desk, Cory Two Trees received a call from Linda. When he answered, he heard her say, "I have a note here that a Mr. Best called when you and BB were out. He wants to talk with you and will be expecting you at his workplace at the end of work, about six thirty."

"Thanks, Linda. Where is BB?" he said into the telephone.

He Heard Linda say, "He went home early. He was sick."

That evening Deputy Two Trees was in the home lighting store parking lot. He saw Carl Best approach his car, open the door and get in. "What do you want to tell me?" he asked.

"I saw the recap of the Connie Brookfield hit and run in the paper. I read it, it is still under investigation but her husband, Brooks, has been arrested for it. Did he kill her?" Carl Best asked.

"It seems so. Surely you didn't call me out here to discuss the hit and run accident. What do you want to talk to me about?" Deputy Two Trees asked.

"I'm not a hundred percent sure, but I studied her picture in the paper and believe she was the woman at the lake," Carl said.

"You mean one of the skinny dippers?" the deputy continued.

"Remember, I wasn't paying too much attention to faces, but I think it was her," Carl replied.

The following morning the upset sheriff was talking to Deputy Cory Two Trees. "I thought it was clear that you were to do nothing or go anywhere by yourself, or after dark!"

"I know, but it was the middle of the day, and BB had gone home sick. What could happen or who would know where I was going? I needed to talk to a witness," replied Cory.

"After work is not the middle of the day! What was so important?" the sheriff asked.

"You said that more evidence on Brooks killing his wife was needed. I talked to my witness about my dead girl when he told me he saw Mrs. Brookfield and Jake Cooke screwing. If Brooks knew his wife was cheating on him it was another reason to kill her. It's not my case but I accidently ran across it and thought you should know," Deputy Two Trees told the sheriff.

Frank Cooper though about what he had just heard. "Thank you for that info but it does not excuse you for disobeying orders, you understand!?"

The deputy put his head down in an apologetic pose and uttered, "Yes."

Chapter 15

Cory and BB walked down a row of holding cells to the interview room. A deputy opened the door and ushered the two deputies in. They saw the handcuffed Brooks sitting at a table. "Brooks, two deputies want to talk to you."

Brooks looked at Cory and recognized him, but not, BB, the deputy with him. "I have nothing to say without my lawyer." Then as an afterthought added, "You here to gloat? Well, go ahead!"

The two sat across the table from Brooks. "No, I'm not, but it is nice to see you here. I'm not going to ask you any questions and you don't have to talk, just listen," deputy Two Trees told the prisoner.

"If you aren't going to ask me questions, why are you here, what do you want?" Brooks wished to know.

"Just wanted to let you know that we have proof that your wife was fucking Jake Cooke," Deputy Two Tree told him.

It got an immediate response, "No! no! I don't believe you!" Brooks was silent as he thought about he heard. "So what?"

"My witness said she liked it and was into kinky stuff," Deputy Two Trees added.

"No wonder you killed her," Deputy BB Larkin said.

Cory knew that they had hit a nerve, so he continued, "She liked it from the rear. She liked to go down on him."

While he waited for a response, Brooks came up off his chair before Deputy Two Trees had time to react, reached across the table and his hands went around Cory's neck. "No, she wasn't! I loved her! I'll kill you, you son-of-a-bitch," Brooks spit out.

It took both deputies Cory Two Trees and BB Larkin to break his grasp. The commotion the three caused brought the deputy guard back into the interview room who saw what was happening. He helped remove Brooks' hands from Cory's neck. "What the hell is going on here!?" He sat Brooks down and addressed the two deputies, "You two wrap it up here. I'm taking him back to his cell."

The two deputies sat for a moment after Brooks was led out. "What was that all about. You don't care about him, why rub it in and rile him. Never though that you were that kind of a person."

"I'm not. Wanted to get a reaction from him and I did. I don't believe that he did it, maybe he truly did love his wife," Cory told his partner and he stood up ready to leave.

"Well, the hit and run is not our case. We have enough to do with the dead girl," Deputy BB Larkin said, and they went out of the interview cell.

Late that afternoon Linda called him and said Carmen wanted to talk to him. When he picked up he told her that he is still working on the case but hasn't made much progress. "I wish I had something more positive to tell you."

He was about to hang up when she said, "I appreciate all that you have done for me and my family. We would like to repay you in some way."

"That's not necessary. I'm sorry about the bad news, but it had to be told. It may sound callous, but that is what I get paid for, part of the job."

"My family would like you come over to my parents for dinner," she replied.

Cory Two Trees was taken aback by her proposal, but he soon recovered. "I don't think that that would be a good idea," he told her.

She persisted, "Why not?"

"For a lot of reasons. It's against policy for us to get personally involved with anyone involved in an investigation, it could cloud our decisions," Deputy Two Trees told her.

"It's a thank you for what you've done for our family. Mom and dad would like to see you."

He hesitated with a response, knew that he shouldn't. "Juan would be all over me. I don't think so."

Then he heard, "Instead of going to our house, I could take you out to dinner," she replied.

"Besides, I am not allowed out at night by myself," he told her, "nor can I drive to your place by myself."

He could hear the disbelief in her voice when she said, "You're not allowed out at night alone. Is that what you're saying?"

"Yes. Without going into details, department policy. The sheriff's decision."

She was quiet for a moment and then said, "I can't believe it, a grown man not allowed out at night, alone."

"Take my word for it. Someday I'll explain it to you," he said to her.

"Well, I've got an idea. I'll drive and pick you up so you won't have to drive. I'll be with you, so you won't be alone," Carmen replied.

The grown man comment caused her to convince him to say yes. He told her his apartment complex and his room number. Said he'd wait at the entrance door. Carmen drove to his apartment building and picked up Deputy Two Trees. He technically wasn't alone and did not drive at night. Both were quiet when she drove them to a restaurant. He turned around and looked through the rear window several times to see if maybe they were being followed. He was sure that they weren't. After several moments, he finally spoke. "I'm not to drive at night or be alone because someone in my past I arrested, maybe sent to jail, has tried to kill me twice. I wouldn't want you to be in harm's way because you are with me should he try again."

"You're sure it's a he?" she asked. "You don't have a jealous woman in your past, do you?" When he didn't answer her she continued, "I'll watch out for the both of us."

He listened to what she said and was sure no such woman existed, and he told her so. In the restaurant, they engaged in small talk. Carmen told him, "I'm glad you accepted my invitation of dinner. You were right, Juan would have tried to create a scene if we had gone to my parent's home, but mom and dad would still like to meet with you. They finally accepted the fact that Angelina had gotten pregnant and was murdered, that she hadn't run away. Want to thank you for what you have done for the family."

Deputy Two Trees didn't know why he thought it, but he did when he said to her, "Maybe Juan is the jealous one. This trouble for me didn't start until after I met you."

"No. This is the first time we have been together and your name has never come up at home. He would have no reason to even think there could be anything between us," was her response. "He never really pursued me. Plus, he has never admitted it, but as I told you, I think he may be gay."

It could be true. Carmen sounded convincing but he would not eliminate Juan as a possible suspect. Angelina's friends believed he was interested in Carmen; it may have been a cover if in fact he was gay. If it were true and Angelina found out, to keep his secret, would he have killed her? It wouldn't explain her being pregnant. No. He could just be protective of the family. He decided to not bring up the subject of Juan again.

Both declined dessert and talked as they ordered a second cup of coffee. "I can't believe that this happened to my sister and I didn't know anything about it. I thought my little sister was pure and innocent," Carmen said.

"A lot of times the family is the last to know. They can't think anything bad about a relative," he said. "Drugs are the biggest culprit."

Carmen just looked at her coffee and continued to stir it. "And she got pregnant. It's so hard to believe."

"I know you never lived at home, but do you have any idea what she might have been doing when she was supposedly babysitting?" he asked her.

"No. She must have been getting money from him. The money covered what she wasn't doing. And the solid gold chain, he must have given that to her also. What should I call him? I can't give him a name," she said.

There was both sadness and anger in her voice. Cory didn't know what to say and said, "I don't know," and he reached across the table took her free hand and held it.

"Why did he have to kill her?"

Cory didn't have to give it much thought when he replied in a low voice, "The usual reasons are money, jealousy or blackmail."

"None of those would apply to her," Carmen replied.

"If what you believe is true, maybe I've been looking at this wrong," was his response.

She perked up when she asked, "What do you mean?"

"My partner, BB, and I have been looking at Michael Morrison, the mayor's son," Cory replied. "Blaming him for statuary rape. Is Michael the wrong guy? Was she killed to protect her real lover, whoever he is? If the guy was found out, what? He'd be ruined, possibly jailed. She could count back to when they began dating, back to when she was thirteen."

When he brought up this possibility Carmen added, "Someone important?"

"I'll have to think about that as a possibility and talk to BB about it," replied Cory.

"Do me a favor?" she asked in a voice that was no longer introspective or self-incriminating but had a tinge of anger to it. So, when he asked her what, she replied, "When you find him, kill him."

Cory was surprised at her response and had to ask, "Are you sure that you would want me to do that?"

Without a moment of hesitation, she replied, "Yes. Shoot him! Kill him! Kill him for me!"

In a calm voice Cory said, "I don't know if I can or should do that. I am the law, and my first responsibility would be to arrest him."

To his response she asked, "Have you ever shot someone?"

"Yes. Once. I didn't like it. I could never do it without cause," Cory replied.

"I could do it. Find the guy and point him out to me," she responded.

He believed she meant it. "Have you ever fired a gun, know how to use one?"

"Yes," she said. "I think so that he could seem manlier, Juan insisted that dad and I should learn how to shoot, keep a gun either at home or in the office. He took us to a shooting range about a half dozen times. I didn't care for it much, but I know how, and I could do it"

"It's a lot different shooting a person than at a paper target. It is extreme and a final resolution to a situation, see blood begin to pool around the body of a man you just shot, you wouldn't forget it," he said.

Carmen thought about what he said for a moment before she said, "You're probably right. I'd like to think I could do it, but I know I never could. Not even to avenge my sister's murder. But you could do it, for me."

"You wouldn't forget it, I haven't. See someone die because of what you did." Cory paused, let go of her hand and suggested that they leave.

When she arrived with Cory at his apartment building she said she would accompany him inside. As soon as they entered his apartment the telephone rang. Cory answered it. As soon as he said hello, he heard his mother say. "I haven't heard from you for a while. Are you okay?"

It was easy to answer her, "Yes mom. I've been kind of busy."

It was going to be one of those phone calls. He heard, "Too busy to give me a call and just say hello. Maybe we could decide on a time when you'd be coming home. I want you to meet somebody."

"Not right now mom, I'm too busy," he said to his mother. "I want you to talk to a friend." He held the phone against his thigh and said to Carmen, "Say hello to my mother. She would like to talk to you." He saw Carmen shake her head no. He held the phone out to her, but she wouldn't take it.

Quietly Carmen said, "No, I don't know her, wouldn't know what to say." Cory held the phone out to her and thought he gave her a pleading look and mouthed please. She gave in and took the phone from him. "Hello Mrs. Two Trees."

Carmen heard Cory's mother say, "You're a friend of Cory's and I don't know you."

"I'm Carmen, Carmen Corilla," she was able to get out.

She heard an excited, "Oh! Cory has told me so much about you. I'm glad to finally get at least to talk to you. You sound so nice. I'd like to meet you."

Not knowing what to say Carmen said to Cory's mother, "Me too. I don't know what to say since I don't know you except to say that Cory is a wonderful man. It was nice talking to you. I'll give the phone back to him," and she held it out.

Cory took the telephone from Carmen and spoke into it, "I don't have much time to talk. I've been really busy with this case and now I must take Carmen home."

His mother was not going to let him go so easily. "I hope she is nice; she sounds like it. Does she like kids? She sounds like she would. You two would probably make a nice family."

Cory hoped she had said enough and he tried to get away from talking to her. "Yes mom. It is too early to talk about that. I've got to go, I'll call you again soon, when I have time."

He could hear his mother smiling when she said, "Goodbye son."

When he hung up the phone he heard Carmen ask, "What was that all about? What's too early?"

He was quick to answer, "She is already talking about Christmas and trying to fix me up with one of her friends' daughters or nieces. Having you talk to her will keep her quit for a while, sorry. I hope you're not upset."

She stared at him. "Did you say yes to my invitation and to come up to your apartment so that you could explain me to your mother?"

"No. I'm not that clever. It was not planned. I had no idea that she would call. Like I said, I'm sorry if I upset you. Come on, I'll walk you down to your car and you can go home."

Next morning the alarm clock set on his radio went off. He reached out to turn it off when an arm went across his body and Carmen reached his neck and kissed him. He turned back to her and kissed her. "Good morning to you too," he said.

"I believed that you'd be a wonderful lover and I was right. Last night was great," she said.

"I've got to get ready for work before BB comes to pick me up," Cory said to her and kissed her again.

In a playful mood Carmen asked, "Did you come up with any ideas last night after we talked?"

"Something came up and my mind was on something else," he said.

"Will you call me tonight?" she asked.

"Yes."

"I'll make us breakfast and you can shower and get dressed. I'll leave here and go straight to work," she said to him.

"You'd better stop kissing me and cover up or it ain't going to happen." At this last statement, she rolled to the opposite side of the bed. He watched her as she began to dress and saw the big smile on her face as she looked at him.

"Okay, maybe no breakfast this morning, but sometime soon."

"Is that a promise?" he asked.

"Yes," was her reply.

They walked down the three flights of stairs. He kissed her goodbye and he watched as she went to her car and drive off. A short time later Deputy BB Larkin showed up and they went to work.

Chapter 16

Cory Two Trees thought about Carmen. He never believed nor did he think that it would happen when he told her yes to dinner. It had not been his intention to get her in bed. But he did. Did he regret it? No. He had, as she said, a wonderful night. As Deputy BB Larkin drove Cory to work he thought about last night. Was it possible that she let him seduce her so when he did find her sister's killer he would shoot him? Did he seduce her, or was it the other way around? He was attracted to her. Was it possible that she felt the same way about him? Only time would tell. It was happening the way he told Carmen, the reason deputies were not to get involved with anyone involved in a case. It could cloud a deputy's thinking. He was already thinking about her, saw her in his mind, could feel her. What was he going to do about her, them?

His thoughts were interrupted by Deputy BB Larkin. "I don't believe it. The state police are going to ask us for help." That morning they were to review the state trooper's auto tape of the shooting.

There was no roll call that morning, but the deputies were all gathered in the roll call room. The sheriff was at the podium. "This is Captain Myers, lead investigator Terry Roberts and sergeant Paul McConnell. They were informed about the hit and run car we found. It is believed that the same car is the one involved in the Jake Cooke shooting. How and why is a mystery, so if any of you see anything on the tape or have a scenario, they want to hear it."

Terry Roberts said to the gathered deputies, "Brooks could have called and report his wife a day before or after the fact, the wrong day. He swears he didn't."

Deputy Fred Smithson asked, "You believe she was killed on the same day Cooke was shot."

"How do you explain that Deer Creek road is nowhere near where the hit and run occurred?" Deputy Susan Black asked

"We believe he may have been fleeing the scene trying to decide what to do with the car," Terry Roberts continued. "He was in a panic, unsure what to do. He knew about the lake and eventually decided to dump the car in the lake. He may have been miles away from the hit and run but, Deer Creek Road does lead to the lake. It was Jake Cooke's misfortune to attempt to stop him and Brooks panicked. Checking on him, Brooks doesn't have a .45 caliber gun registered to him but considering the number of criminals he has defended, he could easily have been given one or know how to get one and keep it unregistered."

Deputy Fred Smithson said, "A search warrant for his home and office turned up several guns, no .45 caliber, but our guys did find a half box of .45 caliber cartridges. State police divers are searching the lake in the area that the car was found. Maybe he also threw it in with the car."

"The empty casing found in the car somewhat backs up our theory. Now all we must do is prove it," Deputy JC Cardozza said.

"Brooks cannot prove he was at home alone working that night. His phone call about his missing wife could have been made from anywhere," Terry Roberts said.

Captain Meyers said, "We've brought a copy of the tape from the scene and hope that one of you may see something we have missed. If you do see something speak up. If you remember anything, contact Sergeant McConnell here or your sergeant."

When there were no further questions, the room was darkened and all eyes were on the TV monitor. Terry Roberts continued to talk as the monitor showed the shooting scene. "As you can see the plates are splashed with what we believe is plain old mud, but the numbers can be made out and were identified. Trooper Cooke's computer showed that he looked them up, they were legit. When we traced them, we found that they had been stolen and had not yet been reported stolen. Cooke got out of his car and you can see him approach the driver's side and motion for the driver to wind his window down. Cooke has his hand near his gun but does not feel threatened by the driver. The window down he leans closer to talk to the driver and puts his hand on the windowsill. He obviously sees the gun pointed at him and shows shock. He didn't have time to react before he was shot. He falls to the road and the driver speeds off. For the next five minutes, there is nothing until the couple who found the body show up. Questioning them, neither remember passing a car before they reached Cooke. The guy goes to the body but too much time had elapsed. Cooke is dead." He has finished talking and indicates that the lights be turned on. "Did any of you see anything or have a question?"

Deputy Susan Black asked, "Is his circling his arm a recognized movement that the widow should be rolled down? If it is not, how did he know that the car had manually wound up or down windows or that the driver would know what he meant by the circling?"

Trooper Terry Roberts answered her, "We believe the driver understood the gesture and the car had electric windows. Even though the cruiser dash camera was not going to show a detailed picture of what happened, our investigation is sure that the driver had turned down or off any interior dash lights so that it was dark in the car. We believe that Cooke's immediate response was shock because the gun could be seen and pointed at him."

Again, Deputy Susan Black had a question, "We saw the trooper's hand on the window ledge, did he leave fingerprints?"

Deputy Fred Johnston answered, "Yes. There was a clear small finger of the trooper."

Deputy BB Larkin asked, "We could see the muzzle flashes on the video, any possibility the driver could be recognized from them?"

"That part was blown up and enhanced by our team. We believe the driver's head was pointed too far away from the window when he shot. Not a clue to who the driver could be. All we know for certain is that it was a man. No way to prove or disprove it was Brooks," Sergeant McConnell replied.

When there were no further questions or comments, Sheriff Cooper stepped to the podium and addressed his deputies. "We are going to be working close to the state police on this. We are going to be looking into the background of Brooks and his wife Connie. What friends or neighbors knew or witnessed. A lot of circumstantial evidence but a good lawyer might be able to cast doubt on it. We need a good solid fact that ties Brooks to both murders. The one piece of evidence that we do have is what Cory reported. He is not working on the case, but he has two witnesses who can verify that Mrs. Brookfield was having an affair with Trooper Cooke. It is possible that Brooks found out about his wife and planned to kill her. What we need to find is evidence that he knew Cooke was the man she was fooling around with. But it would have been impossible for Brooks to know where and when he could find Cooke alone."

"It could just be coincidental that he killed Cooke," Deputy Black said.

"It could be, but we are going to be looking into if Brooks knew about his wife and how he could possibly know where Trooper Cooke would be on that night," Terry Roberts said. "According to Sergeant McConnell, Cooke was randomly assigned to Deer Creek Road that very day. Impossible for anyone to know."

There was some idle chatter among the deputies but no additional comments or questions concerning the shooting of the State Trooper. The meeting was over and everyone went back to their desk or on patrol. Deputy Two Trees walked to the sheriff's office and knocked on the jamb. Sheriff cooper invited him in and asked what he could do for the deputy investigator. Deputy Two Trees knew what he had to do so he readied himself for what he had to say. "I should be taken off the dead girl investigation."

The sheriff believed that Deputy Two Trees was going to be asked to be re-assigned to work on the Brooks investigation, so he cut him off before he could ask and before Deputy Two Trees could ask for a possible exception. "No way. You've made a lot of progress with the dead Corilla girl and taking you off the case, I can hear it now. Mr. Corilla will not accept it and he will let the mayor know about it who will let me know. I said it before and I'm saying it now, you are to stay away from Brooks."

"This has nothing to do with Brooks, but with Carmen, the Corilla daughter. We sort of were attracted to each other and well, had an affair. I've compromised the investigation," Deputy Two Trees told the sheriff. "It is against department policy." He could see the sheriff thinking about what he just heard and waited for an answer. When the sheriff didn't immediately answer, he said, "BB is up to date on where we are. He can more than adequately take over the investigation."

Finally, the sheriff spoke, "I know what policy is concerning a deputy and an investigation. I also know you and believe that you are beyond being influenced by a member of the family, so the answer is no. I am not taking you off the investigation. If you are romancing the daughter I want and expect you to be above any influence and obey the law. Keep an open mind and see the investigation through." Both were quiet for a moment before the sheriff added in a raised voice, "Am I clear!?"

The deputy was surprised at the sheriff's answer but was pleased with it, not so much about not be taken off the case but he was looking forward to seeing Carmen again. "Yes sir! I promise, I will do my best!"

The sheriff called Linda and told her to send Deputy BB in to see him. He looked at Deputy Two Trees and replied to the deputy's response, "You will do your best!" Through the sheriff's door walked Deputy BB Larson. "Tell me, where are the two of you on the dead girl?"

"We are at a standstill. Everyone we've checked on has led us to a stone wall," Deputy BB Larkin answered.

"The two of you keep looking. Go over what and where you've already checked. Bring me something positive," the sheriff said to his two deputies.

"Our only possible guy to look at again is the mayor's son. Right now, he is our only suspect," Deputy BB Larson continued.

"Pressure him. Just do not violate his rights," Sheriff Cooper told them. "I don't want to hear from his father again."

Both deputies almost under their breath said okay, the sheriff was satisfied and dismissed them.

Back at their desks BB Larkin was looking at his notes and Cory Two Trees was on the telephone. Deputy BB Larkin could hear his partner ask, "Trooper Roberts, why was Jake Cooke patrolling Deer Creek road that night? I didn't ask that question when you were here, but now I would like to know." He was silent for a moment and then repeated what he had heard Terry Roberts say, "You don't know why for sure, but that same question was posed by your investigating team?" Again, there was a moment of silence as he listened to what he was told and repeated it for Deputy BB Larkin's benefit, "Sergeant McConnell occasionally assigned troopers to patrol problem areas or the trooper just picked a road. All that they needed to do was call in and say where they were. The trooper on duty said that he had not received a call asking where Cooke might be."

After another moment of silence Deputy Two Trees said, "It's not important, I was only wondering. Thank you," and he hung up his phone.

Deputy BB Larkin followed up with his comment, "It had to be pure coincidence that anyone would know where Trooper Cooke would be."

Cory looked at one of the several cards he had in front of him, picked up his phone and dialed the number on one. "Sergeant McConnell. This is Sheriff's Deputy Cory Two Trees. You said to call if we have anything to add or if we have questions concerning the trooper shooting. Why was Trooper Cooke patrolling Deer Creek Road that night?"

Deputy Two Trees heard the sergeant say, "I'd received complaints from residents along the road about out-of-control speeders. I decided to have it checked out for a few nights."

"Why Jake?" deputy Two Trees asked.

"He was working nights that week and so I gave it to him to check out." Deputy Two Trees heard the sergeant and was quiet after the last statement before he was asked, "Is there anything else deputy?"

"Did you tell anyone?"

"No. If anyone knew it was because Trooper Cooke would have had to tell them."

"Could he have been heard calling in his location?" Deputy Two Trees asked.

"You would need to talk to the night dispatcher, which we did, and he said the trooper never called in. No one could have overheard him on his radio," he heard the sergeant say. "We've checked with his live-in girlfriend and any other women he might have known. Did he call them? Maybe planning on meeting up with them after he got off patrol. All reported that he didn't." He had nothing else, said so, thanked the sergeant and hung up his phone.

Deputy Two Trees didn't ask if they questioned Connie Brookfield, she was dead. He passed the possibility along to the lead investigators on the case that they maybe should check on any incoming calls to the Brookfield phone, and if he did, could it have been intercepted by Brooks Brookfield. It was a possibility that Trooper Cooke had called Connie Brookfield. They did check, found that no such call was made, and it was determined that she had been hit and killed the day before the trooper was shot. Deputy BB Larkin asked, "Well, what did he say?" There was no answer. Back at his desk he repeated, "What did the sergeant and the lead investigators say?"

"Jake was assigned to check out the road for speeders," he replied. "No one would know where he was patrolling unless Cooke told them, and they could find no evidence that he did."

"Why are you asking questions about the shooting? It is not out case and I'm sure the state police have checked out all possible leads. So, the state police knew he would be there, so what? Let's get back to our dead girl," Deputy BB Larkin said.

Deputy Two Trees asked, "Could someone from their barracks be involved? Maybe a friend of Brooks? This friend could have told Brooks where Jake would likely be on that night. So, Brooks raced up Deer Creek road that night knowing that Jake would stop him."

"This person could not have gotten Jake to patrol Deer Creek road, but would know he would be there," Deputy BB Larkin replied as he took an interest in what Cory had just said.

"How do we find who the trooper is who conspired with Brooks and how would we prove it?" Deputy Two Trees asked.

"It's not our case or problem. Pass your theory on to Fred," Deputy BB Larkin replied.

Later the two deputies were in the sheriff's office explaining their progress on the dead girl. "We don't know where to look anymore. We keep coming back to the nights she was supposed to be babysitting."

"We have been unable to come up with a suspect. The guy had to have been giving her money, maybe not for sex, but gave her money to convince her family she was still babysitting. No luck in finding him," Deputy BB Larkin reported. "We keep coming back to the Morrison kid. He and his father has made it quite clear that we can't talk to him without his lawyer."

Sheriff Cooper told them, "Forget about him. Could there be someone else? Someone you may have talked to but do not suspect?"

"For a moment I believed it might be the friend of the family, Juan-Hernando Medina. I dug a little into his background and all his friends, the ones he is close to, believe he is like a part of the family and most can't prove it but, believe that he is gay. Could not, would not ever harm either of the sisters. Never showed or expressed an interest in Angelina. Carmen got an empty soft drink can from him and I had it tested. His DNA proved he is definitely not the father of the fetus.

"A remote possibility," Deputy Two Trees mused, "instead of the Morrison kid, let's take it to a higher level, his father, the mayor. Is it possible that instead of protecting his kid he is protecting himself? Somehow he was introduced to Angelina and hooked up with her? One of her friends told me she had a thing for older men."

The sheriff was surprised when the possibility the mayor could be a suspect was broached.

After a moment of silence, the sheriff said, "Don't go there unless you find some compelling reason to do so! If you do, run it by me first."

They were all quiet for a moment when Deputy Two Trees said, "The only thing that I have is the event at the lake near where her body was found."

"You mean the skinny dippers?" asked the sheriff. "Talk to them again and keep looking."

He questioned both Carl and Denver again separately and alone. Neither could add additional information to their first report to Deputy Two Trees and Denver again made a pass at him. Let him know that she would be available if he was interested. What could they possibly say about the Brookfield woman being killed? He wondered. Nothing except that she and the trooper had had an affair or was having one.

Later Cory said to Deputy BB Larkin, "I keep forgetting about the other car. What if the trooper's car lights revealed who was in the other car? Maybe not his car lights but he recognized the car. It had Angelina and her lover and somehow Jake recognized him."

"If what you're saying is true, it could be the reason why he was killed. He could be jailed or ruined if it became public. And you said Denver was sure Jake was showing off to the other car? Sounds like he knew who was in it," Deputy BB Larkin said.

"I wonder what color the mayor's and his son's cars are?" He found that one was black and the other dark blue.

Chapter 17

Deputies Two Trees and BB could not find anything that could possibly implicate the mayor or his son. Each had an alibi on the nights Angelina was supposedly babysitting unless they were both seeing her on alternate nights. Very unlikely.

On the morning after Deputy Two Trees' theory of who could have shot the trooper, his idea that someone at the trooper barracks was in league with Brooks and somehow found out when and where Trooper Cooke would be on patrol and passed on the information to Brooks. He kept thinking about this scenario. At his desk he asked his partner, Deputy BB Larkin, "How can I get a copy of the out-going calls from the state police without them knowing?"

"It would be easy," Deputy BB Larkin answered. "The telephone company can provide it. Get a judge to okay a request. Why would you want to do something like that?"

Deputy Two Trees explained his theory of the trooper shooting. He saw his partner think about what he said and didn't say anything. Deputy Two Trees said. "If a call to Brooks from the state police could be the final nail in his coffin. Let them look into who may be a friend of Brooks, owe him a favor."

"So now you are not sure Brooks didn't do it?"

"I'm not sure, just having second thoughts. If it were a guy who called about speeders on Deer Creek Road, he couldn't know when Trooper Cooke would be there. He may have called about people speeding which would cause a trooper to check it out. But it would come back to a state trooper letting Brooks know who and when," Deputy Two Trees replied.

"Not if he used a cell phone," and the deputy paused.

"Maybe not. But like us, they tape all calls. The question is, how long do they keep them?" Deputy Two Trees asked half speaking to himself.

"We would have to get their permission to listen to taped calls, not like a telephone number print-out," Deputy BB Larkin said, and added, "let's not overlook the obvious," he added. "If you are going in that direction, the shooter could be a state trooper." Both had come to the same conclusion but both deputies believed that it was a bit too farfetched it would have been another trooper, but Deputy BB Larkin was not afraid to voice it. "It is possible that Trooper Cooke didn't get along with another trooper. Could it be possible that someone he worked with hated him enough to kill him?"

After Deputy Two Trees told Deputy BB Larkin about a possible motive he then told him of his theory concerning a woman with an important person in the car at the lake, especially if Trooper Cooke recognized the woman. Then he added, "She could be an underage girl, our dead girl, Angelina. A girl ten years or more younger than the trooper. All of this is based on something we cannot prove. Who was the guy in the black car? Could it be a trooper and not an important person?"

"Or as you told the sheriff, the mayor? But our checking on him has eliminated the mayor. On the nights of the shooting he was chairing some sort of council meeting that ran till almost midnight. That would leave his son and when we talked to him he was kind of nerdy. Not brazen enough to have done it and our original suspicion and gun check, we found the mayor, nor his son had a registered .45 caliber handgun." They were both quiet for a moment. "We would have to come up with a good reason why we are interested in the trooper telephone log," Deputy BB Larkin replied. "Last thing we would want is to have them believe that the county sheriff's department is investigating them, one of their own. Again, I don't have to remind you. It is not part of our investigation?"

"Let's keep Fred and JC up to speed and take my hunch to them and the sheriff."

The four deputies were in Sheriff Cooper's office, Deputy Two Trees was talking. "We will be looking at someone that possibly set Jake Cooke up or at the least told Brooks where he would be on that night. A friend or someone who owed Brooks a favor. Brooks knew about the garaged ford and how to get to it. The keys were not found and it was hotwired. It's not that easy as you see on TV or in a movie. Did Brooks know how? I don't know, but if someone he defended, a bad guy was told about the car, that guy very well might know how."

"Or not a bad guy, a citizen, not Brooks. Could be someone owed him a big favor and decided to repay Brooks. As you said sheriff, Brooks has a lot of friends," Deputy BB Larkin added. "Could be the guy Jake recognized in the car. If he was, he must be someone very important, especially if Jake also recognized the woman. The guy felt it important enough to kill both Jake and the Brookfield woman."

All were silent while they let what Deputy Two Trees said sink in. Finally, Deputy Jesus Cardozza said, "Boy, the guy must be very important to consider something like that!"

"Or the woman," added Deputy BB Larkin.

The sheriff spoke, "Cory and BB looked into the possibility that there suspect in the Angelina case could be the mayor or his son. The mayor is important enough, but their investigation has eliminated him. His son, Michael, is still a possibility but they have been unable to get very far looking at him. Who was the woman? She may have been the one the shooter was trying to protect. He wasn't trying to protect himself but the woman."

When the subject of the woman came up Deputy Two Trees mentioned that the woman was possibly his dead underage girl. "Not someone important, but someone because of her age would get the guy in trouble, possibly end a career."

"Boy, this is hard to believe. Someone was smart enough to arrange something like this and you think that both deaths are tied together somehow," Deputy Fred Johnson said. "Couldn't be your dead girl though. She was killed before Trooper Cooke saw the second car and who would now be our suspect."

"No." said Deputy Two Trees. "If I look at what I believe is my timeline, the incident at the lake was several weeks before my teenage girl was killed and several weeks after that when Trooper Cooke and the Brookfield woman were killed. Since we are speculating on a motive, why they were both killed, if Cooke recognized the other car occupants, wouldn't he have talked about her, them, to Mrs. Brookfield?"

Everyone was quiet for a moment while they thought about what was said. Finally, the sheriff broke the silence, "Let's keep this secret, it doesn't go outside this office and stays between just the five of us, understand?" There was general agreement among the deputies as the sheriff continued. "We need to know if Brooks ever called the barracks or if someone there called him."

"We have no proof. We don't know which of our important citizens it might involve, maybe a trooper, or did Brooks do it on his own," Deputy BB Larkin told the group.

After the meeting Deputies Jesus Cardozza and Fred Johnston began to investigate the possibility of individuals who may have been indebted to Brooks, his close and important friends, Cory and BB assisted them. It took most of the day and proved fruitless.

The two lead investigators of the hit and run case followed up on calls to Brooks, they found one from an unlisted number that lasted for eight seconds on the evening of the hit and run and the Jake Cooke shooting. Long enough for someone to say Deer Creek Road. When they questioned Brooks, without Deputy Two Trees or his partner BB Larkin who were watching the interview on a monitor, he denied getting a call on that night. They pressed on saying it was long enough for the caller to only say it's done. His explanation was that the call was picked up by his answering machine and it was not him. He maintained that he had been home alone on the night of the hit and run of his wife. There was no mention of the shooting of the state trooper nor that the car retrieved from the lake was involved in both in the event that if he had help, was involved in both, he could warn whoever had helped him. No way to prove or disprove what he told the two deputies, but if he was at home, why didn't he answer the call. His simply answer was that he had been receiving a lot of unsolicited phone calls from unavailable phone numbers so, he wouldn't have answered it and the next day when he listened to messages, it was just dead air and he erased it. If it were an important caller they would either leave a message for him or they would call back. The deputies reported their finding to the sheriff. Either of the two events happened after the eight second phone call and couldn't be proved what the call was about or from whom.

"Could someone wanting to set up Brooks be that clever to place a short call to his home?" Deputy Two Trees asked. After he voiced his opinion they were all silent.

"Who could be that smart to give himself that little bit of added protection?" Deputy Jesus Cardozza asked.

Chapter 18

On Monday morning Deputy Two Trees and BB Larkin didn't ask Fred or JC how they got the telephone printouts. They knew that they were to keep it quiet, not let the state police know they were being looked at or one of their own was being considered in the hit and run investigation and possibly the trooper shooting. The two deputies looked at the print-out of all the state trooper incoming calls for the last month. They saw numbers of callers but no names. Like the telephone numbers of callers to the state police, they had to get an order from a judge for the telephone company to provide the names and numbers of people in the area. The company had no way to isolate only the Deer Creek Road residents. In the event that a resident along Deer Creek Road had in fact called, but didn't want to admit it, it took a long time, but the two deputies cross checked the caller numbers with the numbers of the names and their numbers of Deer Creek Road residents.

Deputy Fred Johnston and his partner were checking numbers called from the state police barracks, could they find Brooks' number. They also had a printout of the numbers called by Brooks. Could they find a citizen that called who was a good friend of Brooks? When could he have called this friend? It was common knowledge that Brooks and the mayor were good friends, but there hadn't been any calls from Brooks to or from the mayor during the time of the trooper shooting.

It took Deputies Two Trees and BB Larkin well into the afternoon before they finished. They found no calls that had come from the Deer Creek Road area. There were a number of calls made from cell phones outside the area and no way to possibly identify who could have made them. It could always be said that one of these callers made the complaint. To be sure, the two deputies would have to double check with all the people that lived along Deer Creek Road, personally interview each household.

That afternoon outside of Deputy Two Trees' apartment, a workman in blue coveralls with a name tag, Joe T., sewn above the right pocket was at his door. He had a dark complexation, could have been Mexican what would be called a stereotype, a full moustache and wore a pair of dark glasses. A hat was pulled low over his head. At his side on the floor was a toolbox. He knocked on the door. No answer. He knocked a second time. Again, no answer from the apartment. On his belt was a ring of keys on a retractable chain. They jingled in his hand as he searched for the correct one to unlock the apartment door. He was not trying to unlock the door; he was picking the lock. He heard the lock tumblers click and he turned the doorknob, but before he opened the door he picked up his toolbox. Inside he took a handkerchief from his back pocket and wiped the knob clean. He put on a pair of latex gloves as he looked around the apartment. He located the bedroom and headed toward it. He set the toolbox down and opened it. From the toolbox, he removed a shoe box and removed its lid. Inside the box was a timer that was attached to a blasting cap inserted into a large lump of gray material. The workman picked up the timer and set it for 'one am', put it back in the box. He waited a moment and watched the digital timer change one minute as it began to count down. Satisfied he knelt at the side of the bed, replaced the lid, and slid the box under the bed. He stood, picked up his toolbox and quickly exited the apartment as he removed his gloves.

That evening Deputy Two Trees was in his apartment sitting in the living room with Carmen. Both had a partial glass of wine. The TV was on, but the volume was very low so that they could talk over it. "I seem to have more success with my case after I discuss the progress with you."

She moved closer to him on the sofa so that his free arm went over and around her shoulder. "I'm good for you, that's why."

"My mother would like you," and he kissed her. "I've gone over all the incoming calls to the state police for the last month. The calls and the interviews with the people who live along the road, there doesn't appear to have been a call, a speeding complaint."

"But you told me their sergeant said there was and that was why he assigned Jake to patrol that road," she replied. The call could easily have been made from a cell phone and there would be no record. Someone who does not live along Deer Creek Road but called to report speeders at night. A call that would get a trooper to patrol it at night, Jake was on night duty and it was assigned to him."

"That's right," he answered her.

Carmen said and after a moment, "And if the caller knew Jake was working nights, very easy for him to be assigned to patrol Deer Creek Road. Didn't need to be from a Deer Creek Road resident, but someone who wanted to set Jake up. A coincidence that Jake and the Brookfield woman were killed on the same night. If you believe that both were killed by the same person, it was lucky for him. If one were killed, and days or weeks later the other killed, who would ever suspect that the two could be tied together, or if even if killed on the same night?"

What she said made sense. They were both quiet for a moment as they thought of what they talked about. Carmen broke the silence when she asked, "Could he be the one? Could the sergeant be the friend of Brooks? Set Trooper Cooke up for Brooks to kill and, he killed them both?"

"It's a possibility, but how does your sister enter into it?" he replied. "I'll think about it." They settled back into the sofa and began to kiss. His hand went under her blouse.

She whispered into his ear, "Remember, I have to get to work early tomorrow."

They are in bed, unaware of the box with its bomb was under Deputy Two Trees' bed. The warning that she had to get up early the next morning seemed to fall on deaf ears. He holds her tight and kisses her. Carmen looks past his shoulder and sees the clock on the nightstand. "Time we were asleep. It's already twelve thirty."

He relaxes his hold of her and whispers okay. They snuggle close to each other and soon fall asleep.

The next morning the sheriff and his investigative deputies are in the roll-call room. He is at his podium and speaks, "You all know what happened at Cory's apartment last night. For those of you who don't, a bomb was placed under his bed. This and the two previous attempts on his life proves that someone was really out to get him. I want to know who and why!"

"Any witnesses?" Deputy Susan Black asked.

"Another tenant in his building saw a repairman going into his apartment in the afternoon and gave us a good description. I want everyone to look at it and see if they might recognize anyone Cory may have had trouble within the past, someone he may have arrested, a friend or relative of someone he jailed. CSI said no prints. The bomb was under his bed and believed to detonate at 'one am' when Cory would be asleep. Killed a tenant in the next apartment and injured his wife. Al Smithson will be investigating the bombing and I've assigned Deputy Lordes to assist him. CSI could find nothing at Cory's. No prints, no idea where the bomb parts could have come from. Whoever is after Cory is now a murderer. I'd like him found and stopped!"

Everyone was quiet for a moment before Deputy Al Smithson said, "We believe that it has something to do with a past case. He and BB are investigating a dead girl and Cory stumbled across a possible connection of a state police trooper, Brooks, and the shot trooper, Jake Cooke."

"It seemed far-fetched, but we told him and Fred to check on it," Sheriff Cooper added. "Cory and his partner were to cross check names of the people who lived along Deer Creek Road. Someone had to get Trooper Cooke to check for speeding on Deer Creek Road. Fred and JC were to look for calls from the barracks that were possibly made to Brooks. After Cooke was assigned to patrol Deer Creek Road, someone had to let

Brooks know which night. Only the state police would know that. And guess who is a very good friend of the mayor, Sergeant McConnell and guess who is a good friend of the mayor, Brooks."

"Unless Brooks sped up and down the road every night," Deputy Susan Black said. "Deer Creek Road is not that well-traveled. Someone could have just driven up and down the road at the posted speed, see the trooper's car and called Brooks."

"That's always a possibility," Sheriff Cooper replied. "A quick eight second call would have been enough."

At the sheriff's mention of his name, after a moment Deputy Fred Johnston began to speak. "Cory has two witnesses that said the shot Trooper Jake Cooke had been having an affair with Connie Brookfield. They apparently saw the two and that Jake was showing off in front of another car at a lover's parking spot at the lake. Cory believed that Jake recognized the car's occupants, for sure the driver. He is someone important and if Jake also knew who the woman was, well if it were to become public who knows what the fall out would be."

He hesitated while the gathered group took in what he said. Sheriff cooper said, "Someone important enough to tell his good friend Brooks Brookfield who decided to act on the information."

Deputy Susan Black asked, "If this person is important enough, and found out that Cory was snooping around where he shouldn't be, maybe he believed that Cory should be gotten rid of also. Killing one more wouldn't bother him."

Sheriff Cooper replied to the Deputy Black's statement, "The two previous attempts would cast doubt on that scenario. The first attempt on his life happened before any of this came to light and how would anyone know about his suspicion unless it came from this office?"

Deputy BB Larkin said, "Here's the kicker, you tell them Cory."

At his request Deputy Two Trees began. "Who would have known that Jake would be patrolling Deer Creek Road? Brooks reached out to a trooper friend who told him when and where Jake would be that night and you know what happened. Or did this important person have a good friend in the state police that told him and he passed it on to Brooks? Could he be an accomplice? If you believe that Brooks did it, someone had to tell him about Jake's patrol area. I told JC this morning, before our meeting, that maybe this good friend of Brooks is in fact the sergeant who assigned Cooke to patrol Deer Creek Road. He helped set a fellow state trooper up."

Deputy Fred Johnston spoke up as soon as Deputy Two Trees finished, "We will be looking at that as a possibility."

When the room fell silent Sheriff Cooper said, "JC and his team are going to begin looking in that direction, Cory and BB are going to get back on their case, the dead girl. Nothing discussed with you this morning is to leave this room, is that clear? Nothing!"

The meeting over, everyone headed back to their areas. When they reached their desk, Deputy BB Larkin had to ask, "How did you miss not being blown up?"

Deputy Two Trees simply answered, "Carmen and I started out at my place but when she reminded me that she had an important meeting with a client the next day, I decided to take her home. Lucky for me that I decided to spend the night there. By luck it was the first time. We will keep our investigation going but I'm not going to forget about the trooper shooting."

Deputy BB Larkin and Deputy Two Trees were to take being baby sat seriously and a deputy in a patrol car was assigned to him at night. He was not to keep regular hours or schedule. That evening Cory was with Carmen in her apartment and he had just explained why a county deputy in his patrol car was parked in her parking lot until Cory entered the building. Cory told her about the shooting of the state trooper. Her response was, "Don't start asking questions without proof or authority to ask them, let those involved in the case deal with it. And, if you're wrong, it could blow up in your face."

Deputy Two Trees replied, "You are right, but I can't stop thinking about it."

"It's a nice night. Let's sneak out, drive down to the lake in your deputy's car, get the interior-colored lights in your car going and forget about the dead trooper case. I'll take your mind off it for a while," Carmen told him. Deputy Two Trees looked at her with surprise and she had to ask, "What is the problem? You don't want to go parking with me and make out? Don't think we can sneak by your babysitter? He left as soon as you entered my building."

"What!? What did you say!?" he asked her.

"Let's sneak out and drive down to the lake and make-out. It's a nice night," she replied.

"No. After that," Deputy Two Trees said.

"I told you to forget about the trooper death for a while," Carmen answered him.

"No! No! About the colored lights!" he said with some urgency in his voice.

"You could turn on the two flashing lights in your deputy's car, but if you don't believe we can sneak out of the parking lot in your deputy car, we can take mine, not yours," she replied.

"That's what Christy said. When he got those colored lights going," and he was silent. He thought about what she had said and replied, "If it was a trooper or a county deputy parked somewhere, their flashing lights would be seen, if only the ones in the car, especially at the lake. Could be reported, questions asked. I believe that several troopers, like county deputies, have internal car lights fitted with flashing lights. It makes it easy for them to drive to a scene without having to go to the barracks for a state car."

"Not if they were somewhere else, where they couldn't be seen, maybe in a garage."

"I hear what you are saying," Cory told her and then about the theory that he had come up with concerning Angelina. For a moment as he thought about what he said. "Damn it! Could it be a law enforcement officer, a state trooper, and Cooke was surprised when he saw him? He recognized him. Not someone who conspired with Brooks, but is the guilty party? He killed all three, your sister, the trooper and Mrs. Brookfield. They all may be separate cases, but somehow, they have a common thread that ties them altogether. What we must do is figure out what it is. It wasn't Brooks at all. He's a convenient fall guy for his wife and the trooper with nothing to do with your sister."

"If what you're saying is true, how does Angelina fit into it?" Carmen asked.

"I don't know," replied Deputy Two Trees.

They didn't go to the lake. Cory was lying in bed; Carmen was asleep beside him. He bolted straight up and awakened Carmen. She could see him in the night light in his bedroom. Carmen touched his arm and asked, "What's wrong?"

"I told you about the video the state police showed us of the shooting. Jake approached the speeder, his hand on his gun, no knowing what to expect. Then he rapped on the car's window and signaled that the driver to roll it down and he leaned closer to the car to see through the open window."

Carmen still partly asleep mumbled, "Of course. He wanted to see the driver's license you said."

"That is what everyone assumed. Jake showed shock when he saw the gun pointed at him," Cory said to her. "What if he was shocked by who was driving and he recoiled, not from the gun, but from the driver, a fellow law enforcement officer," Cory said to her as he talked to her and himself.

There was a moment of silence as the two thought about what he just said. Carmen was the first to speak, "He was killed because of who the driver was, not for speeding."

Cory spit out, "God Damn it!"

"What?" asked Carmen.

"It wasn't a random killing. The driver had planned to kill him," he replied.

Carmen was fully awake now when she asked the same question that Deputy Susan Black had asked, "How did the killer know that Jake would be patrolling Deer Creek Road? It's not that well-traveled."

"I don't have answers to all of the questions, but it all fits together," he replied.

"And Angelina was the girl in the car that Carl and Denver saw," she said. "Jake recognized her and the guy, knew she was a minor. The shooter had to get rid of her also," Carmen replied.

"Angelina was killed a week after Carl and Denver saw Trooper Cooke and close to two weeks later when he was shot. I doubt she was the woman in the car, and if he did kill her, why the crude abortion?" Deputy Two Trees asked, a question for Carmen and himself.

"Did they tell you when they saw the event at the lake?" Carmen asked.

"Yes. And it all fits together except for the abortion. Why would he want to do that? Why not have it done by a professional?"

"Because she was so young, questions might be asked, the police told," was Carmen's reply.

Chapter 19

At work the following morning, Deputy Two Trees' explained to his partner Deputy BB Larkin, the ideas that he and Carmen bounced off each other until they came up with the theory of who shot the trooper. "Should you be discussing the case with her, someone not in the department?" Deputy BB Larkin asked.

"Probably not, but it's too late now. I need to talk to Carl and Denver again. It will be daytime and anyone after me will have no idea what my schedule is or where I'm going. I'll know if anyone is following me. He can't try to ambush me." Cory called both and arranged a time and place to talk to them separately. When he asked when they saw the skinny dippers, they disagreed on the exact date, it could have been a week or more before they first had said, but both were quite sure that it was before when the ME said Angelina had been killed. He was sure that Trooper Cooke would have seen the woman, girl, in the parked car at the lake, recognized her.

"How would the state police know about the garaged car," asked Deputy BB Larson.

Later that day both deputies were in the sheriff's office, Deputy Two Trees was speaking, "Sheriff, BB and I did some checking and found that two years ago the state police were assisting us on a drug dealer sweep. One of the areas searched for dealers who escaped our guys was near the Mary Jennings place."

"The name is familiar but who is she and what does she have to do with what you two are doing?" replied Sheriff Cooper.

"One of the buildings searched by the state police was her garage, the garage the car was stolen from used in the shooting and hit and run cases," replied Deputy BB Larkin.

"I thought that I told you two to get back to your case and the dead girl."

"You did, and we haven't quit looking, but since we are on a roll with the information concerning the shot trooper, we felt it important to keep going," Deputy Two Trees said, "and I have a thread that might tie the two together."

The sheriff was quiet for a moment and then said, "Okay, what's going to tie the two together and what is your next move?"

"Everything we know now points to sergeant McConnell. Somehow, he is involved," Deputy Two Trees said.

"Can you tie him to Brooks or the mayor?" asked the sheriff.

"Not right now, but we intend to keep looking," replied Deputy BB Larkin.

"Let's get Fred and JC involved, see what they think," and he picked up his phone and talked into it.

Deputies Johnston and Cardozza came to his office and were told about Two Trees and BB Larkin's finding. Deputy BB Larkin was the first to speak, "If we believe the sergeant is involved maybe he could have provided the gun as well as the information about Trooper Cooke's patrol area. You never found that Brooks owned a .45 caliber pistol. Now we will need a phone record from the sergeant's house to Brooks."

"Take it a step further. Is it possible that the sergeant is Brook's friend?" the sheriff asked. "What was he doing on the nights the two murders occurred? Does he own a .45 caliber pistol? Find out and get back to me before the end of the day."

Late that afternoon they all checked in with the sheriff. "No luck on where the sergeant was on the night of the hit and run," said Deputy Johnston. "We had to be careful asking questions since the state police have not been told he is a suspect. The only way to find out would be to question him."

"If he has a gun, it's not registered. We would have to search his house," added Deputy Cardozza.

"What about telephone calls Cory?" asked the sheriff.

"Like Fred and JC, no luck. As best we could find was that there were no calls from any of the residents along Deer Creek Road to the state police barracks. We also checked with the residents in the event they may have called from other than their home," Deputy BB Larkin said.

"And we didn't find any calls either to or from Brooks and the barracks," said Deputy Two Trees.

"If none of you can come with anything more incriminating, tomorrow I'm going to have to talk to Captain Meyers and let him know we are going to investigate one of his men," Sheriff Cooper said.

Cory was told by the sheriff that Deputies Smithson and Cardozza would continue their investigation and Al Smithson would continue to investigate Cory's past and look for a possible assassin. Deputy BB Larkin was to watch for potential trouble between Cory and anyone in his past. That evening as usual a sheriff's deputy followed him to Carmen's apartment in a police car. He would be staying at her place for a while until he found a place of his own. Deputy BB Larkin would pick him up in the morning.

Chapter 20

At the end of the day shift, only one investigative deputy would be on duty, Deputy Luke Billings. Since Deputy Two Trees was on an irregular work schedule he was still in the detective room when Deputy Billings arrived. "Are you working overtime?" he asked Cory.

"No. I'll be out of here in a minute. All I have left to do is check any messages on my machine and I'll be out of here," Cory replied.

When he pushed play-back he heard Carmen's message. "I've called Sergeant McConnell and told him I knew what he did to my sister. I said I found his name in her diary. I told him I wanted to meet with him tonight after work at nine o'clock at my apartment. I plan on getting him to confess and tape it. If he doesn't show, maybe he is innocent. Call me later. Bye." Cory was surprised at what he heard. He hung up and immediately dialed Carmen's office number. He heard her telephone message that she was away from her desk, to call back and how to reach her. He talked over the message and waited until it ended and shouted her name to pick up if she was there. He received no response and he decided that she wasn't there. He told her not to meet with Sergeant McConnell by herself. He next called her apartment number and waited through the message on her phone, all the while thinking how dangerous and reckless her move was and left the same message. If the sergeant were the killer that they believed he was, he killed maybe three people to protect his identity, what would one more matter. He had to look through his notes to find her parent's telephone number and dialed it. He hoped that she may have gone home. He talked to her father and told him that if she called or showed up to make her stay there and to call him.

He called Deputy BB Larkin and told him about Carmen's accusation of the state police sergeant. Cory listened as his partner said, "If he did it, is guilty, and believes she knows it, I don't think he will wait until she gets home. He will ambush her sooner. Force her to turn over her sister's diary."

"There is no diary. She wants to meet him after work, she said around nine o'clock," Cory said into the phone. "She said she'd meet him at her apartment. I've tried to call her everywhere she might be. No luck. I'm going to her apartment; I need you to check out her office."

When Cory left the sheriff's building he did not look for or wait for his babysitter, instead he got into his deputy's car and raced to her apartment. He turned on his lights and siren and knew he wouldn't be stopped for speeding. He parked at her apartment and ran inside. He rang the buzzer outside her apartment and then knocked loudly on the door. He called into her apartment several times and waited. Nothing. He thought about kicking the door in when a neighboring tenant who lived across the hall from her came up to him. "She hasn't come home yet. I can usually hear her open her door and I noticed when I drove in, her car wasn't in the parking lot."

He thanked her and turned to leave. As he did, Cory took out his mobile phone and dialed BB Larkin. It rang several times. As it rang he could be heard to say, "Come on! Come on!" Finally, Deputy BB Larkin's voice was heard, "You have reached the telephone of Billy Bob Larkin. I am away from my phone right now but if you leave a message, I will get back to you as soon as possible. At the sound of…" Cory closed his phone and put into his pocket and left the apartment complex.

In his police car Cory took out his phone and hit redial. Again, he heard BB's voice that he was away from his phone. He put the phone back in his pocket. When he got to the parking lot of Carmen's real estate company it was almost empty. He saw two cars and BB's deputy sheriff's car parked several spaces away from Carmen's car. He parked beside BB's car and hurried into the building. At the elevator, he pushed the up button and like when he encouraged BB to pick up, he told the elevator to hurry. Once inside he pushed the three, the doors closed, and it began to rise.

The doors opened and he got off on the third floor. The first thing he noticed was the blood trail on the floor. He pulled his gun and followed the blood. He rounded a corner and saw Deputy BB Larkin lying on the floor in a pool of blood. He bent down and saw his wounded partner move. "BB, it's me Cory."

BB opened his eyes and a slight smile crossed his face. "I'm okay. He surprised me. Never had my gun out. He fired twice when I got off the elevator, one in the leg. I can't move it. Must be broken and one in the shoulder. Thinks he killed me." Cory took out his cell phone and dialed 911, identified himself and told the operator what the emergency was, a wounded policeman and the location. He rang off and told his partner, "Just lie still. I've called for help."

He saw BB wince. Cory pulled off BB's belt and wrapped it around his leg above the wound, pulled it tight and told his partner to keep it tight as possible to stop the bleeding. He pulled BB's shirt off his shoulder as far as he could and tore its buttons off. He saw the wound bleeding and noticed that BB was wearing a vest. It looked like he was bleeding just outside the vest. He pulled the straps loose and exposed the wounded area. He saw the wound bleeding. Cory tore a piece of BB's shirt, wadded the torn shirt and placed the wad over the wound. "I'll hold it as best as I can." BB said as he reached across his chest to the wadded shirt.

Cory took out his cell phone a second time and dialed 911, told the operator again what the emergency was, his location and told the operator to tell the emergency response team to hurry. "Just lie still. I've called for help."

He is quiet for a moment and before Cory can say anything BB said, "He's the state police sergeant and he's got Carmen. I'll be okay Cory. Go get the son-of-a bitch. It hurts. Shoot him for me if you get the chance."

Gun out, Cory peered around the corner. Saw nothing and went to Carmen's office. Tentatively he pushed the door open. He didn't see Carmen or the sergeant but called out to her, "Carmen! Carmen!" He knew that the state police sergeant didn't go back past BB, or BB would have told him. Cory continued down the hallway toward the exit door and tried the doors to other offices that he passed. They all had their doors locked. Almost at the end of the hallway were the rest rooms, men on his left, women on his right. He was against the wall on his left. Before he reached out to push the door open he had his cell phone out and dialed. He heard it answered by the night desk sergeant. "Will, this Cory. I am at two, twenty-four Wedgewood Circle, third floor. I've already called for medical assistance. BB Larkin has been shot and I'm after the shooter. According to BB, the shooter is the State Police Sergeant McConnell. Send help!"

Cory believed the sergeant took Carmen and exited down the stairs; most likely didn't want to see the dead deputy he had shot. Cory needed to check the rest rooms first before he would also exit down the stairs. He pushed the door open to the men's rest room, crouched down and entered. Close to the floor it was easy for him to see under the stall partitions. He saw nothing. Cory stood, gun pointed he pulled the door open as he began to exit. He was intent on checking the women's rest room but didn't notice that its door was ajar, and the barrel of a gun was inside the opening. The shot was deafening as the noise bounced off the hallway walls. The bullet hit the door and splintered it, inches from Cory's head.

Cory jumped back into the rest room and to the side. He pulled the door open and placed his foot between the door and the jamb. He carefully peered through the partially opened door. He could see the women's rest room door open wider and framed in the opening was Sergeant Paul McConnell, his arm around Carmen's neck, a gun held against her head. "Get back! I'll shoot her! Drop your phone!" Cory threw the cell phone through the door toward the women's rest room. "Now the gun!"

Cory heard him and through his mind flashed the idea of giving up his gun and then the image of him and Carmen, both lying on the floor, shot and bleeding. McConnell had already killed four people, because he believed he had shot and killed Deputy BB Larkin. Cory was not going to let it happen, he would call McConnell's bluff. "No way!"

"I swear I'll shoot her!" McConnell said with desperation in his voice.

Cory continued with his bluff and with conviction in his voice, he said, "You do and one second later I'll kill you!"

McConnell didn't say anything but forced Carmen through the door, his hand still firmly around her neck, his gun now pointed at her back. He walked backward with her down the hallway and shuffled toward the elevator. "Stay back!" he heard McConnell say. When they were about twenty-five feet away, Cory stepped out of the men's restroom. Gun pointed at the two, he stayed against the wall and followed. Sergeant McConnell and Carmen approached the shot Deputy BB Larkin. BB pulled his gun out, but McConnell kicked it out of his hand. When they reached the elevator, McConnell reached out with his gun barrel and pushed the elevator down button. The elevator doors opened, and he backed in and pulled Carmen with him. He pushed 'G', the ground floor with his gun barrel and after a few seconds the doors closed.

Cory knew that the state patrolman would in his mind know how the scene was going to play out. All three, Cory, BB Larkin and Carmen knew who he was and now would also believe that Carmen had evidence that he was the one who had killed her sister, Angelina. Escape was futile.

Cory reached shot BB. He heard him say, "Get him Cory."

"Don't talk. Stay still and be quiet. Help is on the way," Cory replied.

Chapter 21

Instead of waiting for the elevator to return, Cory raced down the hallway past the restrooms to the door with an exit sign over it. He pushed the door open and entered the stair well and ran down the stairs. Not sure where the door at the bottom opened to, he cautiously pushed the door open and saw to his right the parking lot. He looked across it and even though it was beginning to get dark, he could see McConnell as he pulled Carmen to his car. He had Carmen open the car door and forced her in and followed. The car started and it raced out of the parking lot.

Deputy Two Trees rushed out through the doorway and ran across the parking lot to his car. He got in, started it, backed out and turned around. He started in the direction that McConnell and Carmen had gone. He turned on his police lights and the siren. He could see the fleeing car ahead of him and it was headed out of the city. He picked up his microphone and called the station. "Will, this is Deputy Two Trees again, I'm in pursuit of the state trooper shooter. It definitely is State Trooper Paul McConnell. We have left Wedgewood Circle and are heading east on Wedgewood Drive. He has a female hostage, Carmen Corilla. Any cars in the area, I need help."

Cory could see McConnell take chances as he illegally wove in and out of traffic and ran red lights as he raced forward. The situation had become dangerous. Cory decided to slow down less the situation deteriorated and innocent citizens were hurt. Soon McConnell's car was out of sight, but Cory kept going. Cory hoped that the fleeing trooper did not turn off Wedgewood Drive. He saw taillights ahead that Cory believed and hoped were Trooper McConnell's. He saw the taillights brighten; he was applying the brakes. Cory was close enough to see the fleeing car blow through a stop sign and turn onto another road. He picked up his mic and pressed to the talk button and called the station again, "Will, we are now heading north on state road thirty-one." He picked up speed so that he was only two hundred feet behind the trooper.

In his rear-view mirror, he could see another police vehicle come up behind him, its lights and siren on. There was no traffic on the highway and all three vehicles were soon out of the city. After they had traveled several miles, Cory could see McConnell's taillights brighten. He was again braking, and he swerved off the state road just past a dirt and gravel road. Cory could see ahead of the fleeing trooper's car's headlights a cable across the road and a 'No Trespassing' sign hanging from it. He had the trooper trapped against the cable. He no sooner thought that when he saw the trooper swerve to the right and he was around the cable. Trooper McConnell had known he could drive around the blockaded road. Cory followed suit. McConnell's taillights were almost totally obscured by the dust the fleeing car stirred up. Cory slowed down because of the unevenness of the road. If he bottomed out going too fast over large ruts he might have to stop the pursuit. McConnell wasn't going too far, Cory believed there was no way out of the farm McConnell was driving to except for the way in, the road he was on.

Cory called the station again. "Will, Cory here. The fleeing trooper has turned off the state road, drove around the cabled off dirt road and is heading up the dirt side road toward the abandoned Kopchek farm." Cory and the police car that followed him arrived at the farm in a cloud of dust and they stopped, their lights aimed at the old farmstead. Where the police cars were positioned McConnell would not be able to leave. If he tried to drive around the two lawmen's cars, he would have to drive through a heavily wooded area. As the dust settled Cory saw the road circled back to itself so that it could service both the farmhouse and the barn. McConnell car was nearer the barn. Cory's car was positioned so that its headlights lit up the house to the east side of the circle, his flashing police car lights temporarily lit up more of the house as they flashed on and off. The car lights showed the house was old and falling apart. Weeds and ivy were overtaking it. Its one-time grassy yard was now overgrown with weeds and small trees as they tried to reclaim it. The roof had fallen in on part of the house, its siding in several places had fallen off or slipped and revealed the two-by-fours studs. From the front, all the windows had been broken. Opposite it and close to a hundred feet away, the accompanying police car was a state trooper's and aimed at the barn, and close to it, Paul McConnell's car. The barn was in the same abandoned and falling apart condition as the house. The state trooper cruiser's flashing lights bounced off the barn and showed how big the barn was and its dilapidated condition. Several of its vertical boards were missing and revealed they were further apart where the narrower boards that had been attached to cover where they butted one to the other, had fallen off. The barn leaned to one side, ready to collapse like the house roof. Its large door had fallen off a broken hinge so it was at an angle as it leaned against the barn. Facing them would have been a large black hole if the cruiser lights didn't shine through the opening to reveal some of the inside of the barn. The slant of the barn and the missing door made Cory think the barn was grinning. Near the barn was an assortment of rusted and broken pieces of farm machinery with weeds partially obscuring the pieces of machinery. The weeds continued to surround the barn and grew up to its edge and several feet into the barn door opening, the distance the sun could reach through the door.

Cory exited his vehicle and in a crouch moved behind the state trooper's car. Both men had their weapons out. "He's most likely in there," Cory said to the trooper and indicated the barn opening.

The trooper said to him, "Name's Barry. I heard you on the radio. Are you sure it is Paul McConnell?"

Cory didn't hesitate to answer, "Yes, it's him. Saw him at the state police briefing. He also has shot my partner." He waited a moment because he didn't want to acknowledge the fact that McConnell had

Carmen before he told the state trooper, "He has a female hostage, Carmen Corilla."

"I know him. I'm going to try and talk him out. Let me talk to him. I'll walk at an angle from my car so that my video dash camera will be able to catch us both." Barry said and Cory saw him stand, holster his gun and walk around to the front of his car with his hands out to his sides. He called McConnell, "Paul, this is Barry. I'm coming toward you," and he reached to his holster, pulled out his gun and held the butt with his thumb and fore finger. "I'm not armed, see." With his last statement, he dropped his gun on the ground. "I'm coming to you. No one wishes to harm you." He took several steps toward the barn and waited. There wasn't a response from the barn. Was it possible that McConnell and his hostage were not in the barn? But Cory heard Barry continue to plead, "Please Paul. Talk to me." He stopped and waited when he was fifteen yards from the barn opening.

Paul McConnell appeared in the doorway with his arm around Carmen's neck, his other hand held a pistol to her head. "Don't come any closer!" he yelled.

Barry answered him, "All I want to do is talk. We go back a-ways. Talk to me Paul." The trooper with Carmen didn't respond. "You know me and my family. You've played with my kids. As a friend, let me help you Paul. Maybe there was a reason for what you did."

"He saw me with her. Probably laughed about us with that woman he was with. He reminded me about it when no one was around. Out of the side of his mouth he would say, twelve will get you twenty. No need for an explanation," Paul replied.

Keep him talking Cory thought. It was possible Barry could talk him into giving himself up. He heard Barry say, "Talk to me. What happened?"

Paul hesitated but eventually said, "I had to get rid of them, both him and that blonde he was with. It took me a while before I was able to find out who she was, the Brookfield woman, but I did it"

"Saw you with who?" Barry asked.

"Angelina. I didn't mean to kill her," Paul blurted out. "I loved her, wanted to take her away. Marry her. Told her we'd raise the baby, be a family. She laughed. She would not leave her family, marry me. She would stay here and have the baby. When it came out who the father was, I'd be ruined, sent to prison. I couldn't stand the thought of being sent to prison. I begged and begged and somehow it just happened. My hands were around her throat and she was dead. I didn't mean for it to happen." Paul stopped, and then added, "the baby tied me to her, I couldn't deny it." Then in a sad voice he said, "I had to get rid of it also. It was the worst thing I've ever done in my life, cutting her open." Cory thought he could see a tear running down Sergeant McConnell's cheek.

Barry said to him, "A good lawyer can help you. Don't let it end like this. Let her go, put the gun down and come with me."

There was a note of sadness in his voice when Cory heard him direct his next statement to him, "I hate you deputy, hate you for what you made me re-live. I couldn't forget her and what I did."

Carmen immediately picked up on McConnell's statement. She tried to turn toward him and in a pleading voice she said to him, "Angelina would not want you to do this."

Cory focused on the gun the sergeant held. He hadn't paid much attention to it back at Carmen's building but now he did. It looked like a .45 caliber automatic. The hole at its end looked bigger than life and when he turned it to point at Carmen, it was very threatening and intimidating. Cory could see a determined look on the sergeant's face. Was he going to shoot her?

When he heard Carmen mention Angelina, McConnell relaxed his hold on Carmen. It was her cue to smash down on his foot with her heel. The startled man responded with a light yelp and at the same time loosened his grasp of Carmen so that she was able to break free and make a dash to the state trooper's car. If Sergeant McConnell would shoot her, Cory would kill him. He grabbed her and pulled her down behind the car. If he wanted to, now would be the time to shoot McConnell. He was in the open by himself and Barry was out of the line of fire. No. He would wait and see what Barry's pleading to McConnell would yield. Barry continued to talk to his friend the sergeant, "I'm going to come to you Paul," and he took a step toward the man who had only recently held Carmen hostage. When he did, Paul pointed his gun at his own head.

Cory believed that McConnell was going to kill himself. "Paul don't do it. It's not worth it. I'm going to come to you," continued Barry and he took a tentative half step. "We are friends, we trained together. You've spent time at my house." Cory could see a determined look cross McConnell's face. For sure, he was going to shoot himself. "Please Paul, as a friend, put the gun down," pleaded Barry who was now close to ten feet from him. A look of calm replaced the determined look on his face and he pointed his gun away from his head. Cory believed that Barry had talked him into giving up. The scenario would have a happy ending. Cory watched as McConnell began to lower his gun and now all he had to do was drop it. Instead in a split second he aimed his gun at Barry and quickly pulled the trigger twice. Before the sound of the second shot had died down, Trooper McConnell had turned and was inside the barn door opening. Cory quickly fired two shots at the opening, but the trooper was out of sight.

What to do Cory thought. Could he go after McConnell or should his first move be to see how badly the state trooper had been shot. Could he help him? "Stay here Carmen, help should be on the way." Cory got on his stomach, kept his gun out and aimed at the barn opening and began to inch on his stomach to Barry. He hoped McConnell wouldn't show himself again. He reached Barry and saw that he was alive. "Don't move," he told the state trooper, "help should be here soon."

"I'm okay. One in my shoulder and somewhere in the stomach. They hurt but I'll live. Sorry, I tried. Leave me and go get him," Barry said. "If possible, as a favor, don't kill him."

Should he crawl back to the state trooper's car? He was close to the barn, maybe make a break for it before McConnell could shoot again. Cory wasn't sure of the decision he made was the correct one, but he was up and zig-zagged quickly to the barn. He stopped near the opening, his back against the leaning door. He made a quick look around the edge of the door opening, then darted inside and hugged the barn wall. Shafts of light from the cruiser showed that dust was inside the barn, either what their cars had made hadn't settled down or it was dust McConnell had kicked up.

The interior of the barn had hay scattered on its wooden floor. In the dark barn Cory could make out more abandoned farm equipment and falling apart animal stalls. He kept low to the floor and moved to his left and tried to stay out of the beams of light that came through the barn's many missing boards that covered the larger barn boards where they met, edge to edge. The beams were narrow but if McConnell were looking he would be able to see Cory when he passed through them. Cory made a dash for an abandoned wagon of some sort and crouched behind it and he peered into the barn's darkness. The head lights from the state trooper's car seemed to be overpowered by the car's flashing red and blue lights and it gave Cory a strange feeling that he was seeing something that was not real. He immediately thought back to what Cindy had told him, that Angelina had said about when he got those colored lights going he was unstoppable. Is this the place he brought Angelina? The trooper knew enough to drive around the blocked off road. Cory waited until he felt that his eyes had adjusted to the barn's darkness. When he moved he could hear the floorboards creak. He heard a noise in front of him. He laid down and looked in that direction. He saw nothing and then felt something run across his legs. He inched forward. Ahead he saw what he believed was a stack of old tires. Up on his feet he broke and ran to them. He was two steps from them when the floor gave way beneath his feet and he fell through the floor. His vest had stopped him from falling completely through. Not knowing that his immediate reaction was to put his arms out to break the fall. When he did, Cory lost the grip he had on his gun. It was somewhere in the darkness hidden in the hay. In a split second, various thoughts raced through his mind. His thought that he had to get out and find his gun. When he moved to do so, he realized how serious the fall was. The floorboards broke down and several had punctured his thigh and crotch. When he attempted to pull himself up, several of the broken boards were pushed further into where they had punctured his crotch and it hurt. Hurt very much. Cory would have to wait until help arrived or he could pull his arms in close to his body and force himself to fall through the floor break. What was down below? He didn't know. What he knew and could feel was blood running down both legs. Funny, he could feel the blood but not his legs. Where was the pain? A quick decision was to fall through to whatever was below.

In the darkness he heard behind him, "I know who you are." Cory had been looking in the wrong direction, the sergeant had turned to his right in the barn, not left, the direction Cory had pursued. He tried to twist his body so that he could face Paul McConnell. And now it hurt, hurt too much as he struggled, and he had to stop trying to turn around. The only thing he could do was turn his head and was able to look over his shoulder. Just outside the police car light coming through the doorway stood the sergeant. "Why couldn't you leave it alone? She would have been missed but after a while would have been forgotten." Cory's outstretched arms began to feel around for his dropped gun. If he did find it, could he turn enough to shoot McConnell? It didn't matter because he couldn't find his gun. He saw McConnell take a step closer to him. "I missed three times, but not this time. I'll make you pay!"

Try to buy time Cory thought and asked the sergeant, "Why the lake and not here?"

"She liked the lake; it was her favorite place. Even though on a blanket, she sneezed when we came here," McConnell said. "She liked the colored police lights my car made as it passed between the spaces of the barn."

"She really loved you. Her sister told me," Cory said to him. He could see McConnell silhouetted from the car lights. If he only had his gun.

"I really hate you for what you made me re-live, keep me from forgetting about her, us. What I had to do. What I did," McConnell replied.

A last desperate plea came from Cory. He tried to play upon the sergeant's love for the girl. "Angelina wouldn't want you to do this." He focused on the gun and the determined look on McConnell's face. There was no doubt at all, he was going to shoot Cory. When he shot him, Cory wondered, would he then go after Carmen and maybe finish off the state trooper? Cory forgot about how hurt he and was beginning to feel pain. He thought that the muzzle hole looked bigger than when he first saw it. The shot was deafening. Cory should not have been able to hear it, but he did. How? Why? He still looked at McConnell who stood there, his gun now at his side and as he watched the sergeant he saw the sergeant's hand let go of the gun and it fell to the floor as he began to fall over. As he fell Cory could see Carmen behind him in the barn doorway. She held the shot trooper's gun, and he could see tell-tale smoke coming from the gun's barrel. He watched as McConnell fell to the floor and raise a cloud of dust. The last thing he remembered before he passed out was the scream of police car sirens and the trooper's police light beams coming through the board spaces be overpowered by the white lights of police cars.

Chapter 22

Cory was in a hospital bed. Standing near him was Sheriff Cooper. The first words that the sheriff asked was how Cory was feeling. Cory's groin area and stomach were sore, but he was alive. "I'm okay but a little tired."

"Doc says you should be up and around in a few days. Nice work solved three murder cases all at once. Between what was on the trooper's video cam, and what Barry and Carmen said, it was all clear as who did it and why. Forensic went over the barn and found where he killed the girl. Not sure why he took the chance of transporting her and the fetus to the lake even though he said she liked it. He could have been seen. We believe that he buried the girl first and either at the same time or later he tried to find where he buried her and couldn't find the spot because it would have been dark. So, the fetus was buried or hidden away from the body. The one perfect slug from Trooper Cooke was matched to his gun. No evidence except the tape as to why he killed the Brookfield woman. A commendation is in store for you. I heard that Brooks is even thankful to you. Most likely won't admit it though."

Cory interrupted him when he asked, "What about BB?"

"He's a couple of rooms down the hall. You should be able to visit him," was the sheriff's reply.

"How bad off is he. All I've been told is that he is alive."

"He's good. One in the shoulder, just to the side of his vest. Other hit him in the leg, broke the femur bone. Doctor said he most likely will be walking with a limp, but BB said he wants to come back to work."

The sheriff paused for a moment before he added, "Said he wants to partner with you. I hope you both will return. The shot state trooper will be okay. He was hit twice but, lucky for him both were superficial, flesh wounds."

Cory wasn't sure what happened after he fell through the floor, he had to ask, "What about Carmen?"

"She is okay. Lucky for you she was there and you're alive. No doubt from her statement and what could be seen and heard on the trooper's video dash cam, the sergeant was going to kill you. She is either a good shot or was extremely lucky, hit him in the neck We hooked her up with our shrink. She will help but her initial response is that Carmen will be okay with what she did. Only time will tell if she needs further counseling."

Cory was glad to hear about Carmen and his next question concerned Sergeant McConnell, "And the sergeant?"

"He's dead. As I said, the bullet hit him in the neck. Shattered his spine. Killed him instantly."

Both men were silent for a moment. Cory didn't ask what he wanted to know but finally got the words out. "Tell me what I really want to know. The doctor won't tell me, says I have to wait and see."

Sheriff Cooper looked at Cory and said, "Told me the same thing. When the floor broke, you went through it and was stopped by your vest. Between the broken wood going down and your twisting as you tried to get free, splintered wood went into your stomach and scrotum. For sure, your balls were damaged. The doctor doesn't know to what extent. A family is questionable. Only time will tell."

It was Christmas much later at the home of his mother, Helen Two Trees. The room was decorated and a lit tree was in the corner with unopened gifts around it. Gifts already opened were scattered around with torn wrapping paper. Cory scurried around as he tried to gather up the torn paper and attempted to stuff it into a box. He was hindered by a German Shorthaired Pointer who ran around and tried to help as the dog grabbed paper and tore it up. It took several minutes to finish the task. The dog was distracted when she was handed a wrapped dog gift that it quickly was able to tear the paper off, but now it was stopped by the plastic wrap around the dog toy, a hard rubber bone. Finally, the dog pulled the plastic off and it had the toy in its mouth. The dog took the toy to the side, laid down on the floor and began chewing on it.

Cory's mother sat near the tree, picked up another wrapped gift and read the name tag. "To Brandon from Mom and Dad. This one's for you," and she handed the gift to Brandon. She held up a second gift and said, "This one is for Holly, from Grandma." She handed the gift to Holly. By this time, the dog had had enough of chewing on the toy and trotted to Brandon to help him tear open his gift.

Brandon tried to push the dog away which seemed to excite it more. He yelled, "Dad, call Calie!"

Cory sat on the sofa, slapped his thigh and yelled at the dog. "Calie! Come here!" The dog paid him no attention. He clapped his hands to get the dog's attention and his second attempt proved just as useless. When he saw that his command to the dog failed, seemed to fall on deaf ears he said, "Hon, she listens to you. Call her."

Carmen smiled and in a calm but demanding voice said, "Calico, come here!" Everyone in the room saw the dog leave Brandon and trot to her and lie down.

The End